LETTERS IN THE LOFT

TOM - tio do Bryan

Helen - esposa TOM, refinada

Pearl; Ted - irmãos de TOM

GORDON - vizinho HELEN

PAUL - filho DELC

Andrew - filho maggie e Brian

LUCY
JAMES   & Abby - namorada

LETTERS IN THE LOFT

Christine Follett

ATHENA PRESS
LONDON

LETTERS IN THE LOFT
Copyright © Christine Follett 2005

ISBN 1 84401 542 4

First Published 2005 by
ATHENA PRESS
Queen's House, 2 Holly Road
Twickenham TW1 4EG
United Kingdom

Printed for Athena Press

About the Author

Christine Follett was born in London in 1947 and qualified as a nurse at St George's Hospital in 1968. She subsequently married and had three children and then worked for seven years with deprived young people, and for a further seven years as a counsellor in a girls' school in Surrey.

She now has three delightful little granddaughters and she has recently moved to Ruislip with her husband and two dogs.

Letters in the Loft is her first published novel.

Acknowledgements

My thanks to my wonderful husband, Christopher, my daughter, Lorna, and sons Jonathan and Richard, without whose love and support this novel would not have been written.

Prologue

Every family has them... secrets, I mean. Sometimes they don't come to light until years after the secrets happened. Ours turned out to be a whole chain of secrets, and we didn't know about any of them until long after Aunt Helen had died.

In fact, until then we thought we were just an ordinary family, with a few of the usual interesting skeletons hidden away along the years, but nothing of the festering sort you might say. Perhaps the mystery began after Aunt Helen's death, but then it lay buried for another eight years until Gordon's demise.

We were eating macaroni cheese by the fire when the telephone rang. It was a cold January evening, and the wind was particularly strong, howling across the patio and lashing the bare branches of the willow tree against the French windows. The dogs were sitting at our feet, hoping that some cheesy fragments might drop their way.

'I'll get it; probably Andrew.'

Brian was expecting a call from our eldest son, whose business was suffering financial problems. I flicked the remote control to 'mute' so as to silence *EastEnders* and overhear this end of the conversation. The telephone was in the hall, and as Brian left the room he pulled the sitting room door closed behind him. I strained my ears to hear. Getting up would have meant moving Millie, who was lying across my feet, warming them while waiting for cheese.

'Right... yes, thank you. Tomorrow then. Yes. Goodbye.'

Obviously not Andrew. Brian returned, looking grave.

'It was the hospital,' he told me; 'Gordon died an hour ago. I have to fetch the death certificate and register it and so on, tomorrow.'

He returned to his supper, but his appetite had gone, and he pushed pieces of macaroni around his plate with his fork, his thoughts elsewhere.

'Poor old boy; no one there with him at the end. Sad state of affairs.'

'Not surprising, I'd say' I commented. 'So it was pneumonia, then?'

'The nurse didn't say, but I expect so. It'll be on the certificate tomorrow, I should think. Loads more work for me now. What a week, eh?' He sighed, and pushed his plate away unfinished. 'Some for you after all, boys.' We often called the dogs 'boys' or 'girls' in the plural for ease, though they were one of each, and they never objected.

Routinely, Brian made the coffee after supper, which I always cooked. Such creatures of habit we had become, just like his parents before us. Ted and Maud had always eaten cheese on toast on Saturday evenings – probably without fail for most of their sixty-two years of marriage. It was the source of much family amusement – kindly meant, that their shopping list remained the same every week and Ted ate one square of Cadbury's Dairy Milk chocolate and half an apple every evening at 9 p.m. until he died aged ninety-three. Possibly becoming creatures of such fastidious habits gave them longevity; something perhaps to be copied.

Brian and I, however, were not like his parents in most ways. We had married young and produced three children within the first four years of our marriage; all of whom were a tremendous delight, and their baby days and childhood were golden years for us all. They had all grown up, married, and thrilled us with two little granddaughters in recent years. Now we rattled around in our large house in Ealing like peas in a drum, waiting, I suppose, for their visits, when the rooms were filled once more with noise and laughter, mess and pleasure. Perhaps more for me than for Brian, my family was my treasure. He still had his work, which occupied his days in our home office, and filled his mind with things more pressing, apparently, than fish pie with the children's favourite pasta, or fairies that came in the night and left hairslides when you were good. Always a financial man, ex-bank manager, ex-financial director of his own business, he now worked part time as financial officer for a charity. Retirement was something other people took early, to enjoy and relax... Brian worked. Always a good man, totally honest, trustworthy and reliable, everyone called upon him to give help and sound advice. And two years before, our eldest son Andrew had come to him, asking for his father's opinion about a new venture. As a result, he sold his flat and embarked on his life's dream of owning a leisure and fitness club, which he built from scratch in Wimbledon. Brian shared his vision, and carefully planned ahead for the finances of this project, investing a large sum of money into the establishment of the gym, which Andrew was to repay when it was successful.

Recently, however, things had turned sour, and the gym was floundering financially. The building works were proving to have been done badly, and Andrew's profits were all being used for repairs and essential maintenance, producing large unforeseen bills.

'We'll come through this, Mags,' Brian would say. Times were the hardest we had known, and work filled our days.

And now Gordon had died, and Brian was his executor, which meant more work ahead. Little did we know then just how much more…

Gordon Lench, ninety years old, widower of Barnes, was an unlikable man to say the least. Fair to say, I think, that no one held him in affection except his beloved cat, who in turn was the only living thing to receive any form of respect from Gordon for many years. A man to feature predominantly in my story, I had known Gordon Lench only remotely since my marriage to Brian thirty-six years before. Brian, however, always kind, had featured in Gordon's latter years as one of the few people who had helped him, or even cared about him to any degree. It was indeed a mystery to us that he had so few friends, but as the secrets of his past unfolded, we were to discover why.

Chapter One

How often my memory brought treasures when I was busy... usually busy thinking, that is. I loved to conjure up pictures of special times, places, people from the past, and just remember it all. Brian's Uncle Tom, however, was always a little fuzzy in my mind, never feeling that I knew him at all well.

Tom Fawley was the eldest of the three children born to Brian's grandparents, and he was always the one the family held in high regard for his academic prowess and subsequent honour in his career. School head boy, captain of cricket and rugby, Oxford boxing blue and high achiever at university, Uncle Tom met Helen Bishop at the tennis club in Sheen when they were both twenty-one years old. He had already begun an eminent scientific career, having gained a 'first' at Oxford and found a splendid post in London in research. She was working in the Bank of England and living in East Sheen with her mother and stepfather, her own father having died when she was young.

Aunt Helen always fascinated me. When I first met her, Brian and I were about to be married. His mother told me that Aunt Helen was a bit odd; 'Very well to do, and not like us really,' she said.

The Fawley family was warm and friendly, welcoming to me, and open and honest. I was surprised to find that Uncle Tom and Aunt Helen were a little 'on the edge' of the family, so to speak, and Aunt Helen especially seemed remote, and kept herself at arm's length from us all. Uncle Tom was also a cool character I found, ready with a smile whenever we met, but definitely distant. And yet the tales of his childhood with his sister, Pearl, and his brother, Ted, proved him to be very different in the years before I knew him.

Our wedding photographs showed them as a distinguished couple; she wearing very grand clothes and he in top hat and tails. There was little apparent affection between them, which surprised me as they had lost three sons during their marriage, and now had only each other. I was intrigued by them, but Brian seemed to know very little when I asked.

'That's just how they are,' he said. 'You'll understand more when you see the house. Aunt Helen is a bit weird... probably since Malcolm died or something.'

'What happened?' I asked.

'He killed himself when I was ten,' Brian said. 'I don't know why; it was all hushed up as I remember, and Louise and I weren't allowed to ask, or mention him. I don't really remember Malcolm, he didn't exactly feature much when Louise and I were kids.'

'How awful... no wonder Aunt Helen's remote. And you say there were two other children that died as well?'

'You'd better ask Louise, or Mum. I think they were twins, but before Malcolm came along, so I never knew them. Died as babies, if I remember hearing rightly.'

I felt great compassion for Aunt Helen, and thought that nothing could be so dreadful for a woman than to lose three children and never be able to mention them or remember them with her family.

We went to visit. It was the early days of our marriage, and we were driving to Barnes to deliver a parcel for Uncle Tom from Brian's parents. We were invited to tea.

'Is this dress all right?' I was anxious to be 'correct', as we were to be in Aunt Helen's company.

'Bit short, I should think,' was Brian's reply. 'Pull it down if you can.'

Ridiculous. This was 1969 and skirts were super-minis. And in those days my knees were great.

We drove to Gumber Lane in Brian's old Triumph Herald on a sunny Sunday afternoon, and parked at the end of the lane by the river. Large elm trees lined the road and the dappled sunshine shone on the pavement. We could hear the swish, swish of rowing blades as boats passed by on the water, practising for the University Boat Race the following weekend.

'What a pretty road,' I commented, and Brian grinned, as I combed my hair ready for inspection on arrival.

'Wait till you see Elmwood!' he said.

'Elmwood' was the house at number three, Gumber Lane, where Uncle Tom was staking runner beans in the side garden. He wore old corduroy trousers tied around the middle with a piece of fraying string; quite a surprise for one so wealthy. I noticed that although he smiled gently on our arrival, he shook our hands formally, and there was no kiss on the cheek for his new niece-in-law.

'Come in, come in,' he said. 'Excuse the gardening togs. Helen's inside preparing tea. Good of you to deliver the books from Ted. How are they both?'

'Well, Uncle Tom, thanks. And you two?'

Brian, I could tell, was not relaxed and comfortable here.

Aunt Helen was arranging tiny cucumber sandwiches on a beautiful porcelain plate in the sunny breakfast room. We were to have tea in the drawing room, where I discovered three cats of differing colours arranged on the blue velvet chairs. Aunt Helen introduced them proudly.

'This is Susie, and Benjy and Plum. All strays, you know, but look at them now. They're my babies, you see...'

The cats were indeed beautiful, tended clearly with the greatest of love and care. Aunt Helen relaxed as she petted each one, and made a space for me to sit down.

'Do you like animals, Maggie?' she asked eagerly.

'Oh yes, very much. I lost my dear old dog just before our wedding, and I miss him terribly!'

Plum, a ginger male, made his way cautiously on to my lap and clawed gently at each of my nyloned knees.

As I looked around this beautiful room, I noticed an array of splendid silverware, neatly arranged on inlaid tables with cabriole legs, and a Cumberland design George III table was laid with a delicate lace cloth and tiny cups and saucers for our tea.

In the corner of the room stood a magnificent grandfather clock with a painted moonphase dial.

'My mother's family clock,' Aunt Helen said, watching my eyes scan the furniture, 'and the piano too... I learnt to play that as a little girl.'

On top of the piano I saw a black and white photograph in a

silver frame, of a young man closely resembling both Aunt Helen and Uncle Tom, whom I presumed to be cousin Malcolm. Something stopped me from mentioning him however, most unlike me, but I must have been becoming a true Fawley already.

That first visit to Elmwood has stayed in my memory ever since. I can remember the scent of the honeysuckle in the ivy hedge; the impression the furnishings in the house left upon me, and the dainty china on which Aunt Helen served our tea. It was all beautiful, but I didn't feel warmth there. I was used to a loving family home where friends and family were welcome at any time without invitation, and there was no necessity to use perfect bone china or delicate silver teaspoons for afternoon tea.

'My family would have called you 'dear,' I said to Brian later, as we lay in the grass by the river. We had driven away from Gumber Lane and parked further along the riverbank in a secluded spot beyond the end of Elmwood's long garden.

He huffed, and pulled strands of dry grass from my hair.

'I told you,' he said, 'that's just how they are. I don't feel I know them very well, really. Funny, I suppose, considering Dad and Uncle Tom have always been close. But Aunt Helen… d'you know, she never comes for Christmas? It's always Uncle Tom who comes alone to our home for Christmas lunch with all of us, and then he goes back to Elmwood for another turkey meal in the evening, which Aunt Helen's been cooking. Like I said, a bit odd really.'

'I suppose she won't leave her cats. Perhaps that's it.'

Brian shrugged.

'There's always one in every family,' he laughed.

'Such a lovely house,' I said. 'Beautiful furniture… I know real antiques when I see them. Where does all that money come from?'

'Well, it's mainly Fawley stuff I think, Uncle Tom being the eldest son. All of the Fawley silver is there I know, and the family clock.'

'I thought Aunt Helen said that was her mother's.'

'Yes, but there's the Fawley family one in the dining room as well. Quite a bit of the furniture probably came from her home, but most of it belongs to Uncle Tom, I'm sure. And of course he

16

cavaline
educado ALONG? AMONG?

has a brilliant job at the Physical Science Institute. You don't get a knighthood for nothing.'

The previous July, in 1967, Uncle Tom had been knighted for services as Director of the Physical Science Institute in London. It was the source of great family pride that Sir Tom and Lady Fawley were related to us. Brian's parents had a framed photograph of them at Buckingham Palace, looking very grand, on the coffee table in their lounge. I had previously wondered whether this great occasion had been a reason to set them apart from us, moving as they must have done amongst select social circles and attending constant functions rather than family gatherings, but Brian thought otherwise.

'Uncle Tom still holds his gardening trousers up with string,' he'd laughed. 'No, they've always been the same.'

The revelation that Malcolm had committed suicide stuck in my mind. There were no pictures of him in evidence at Brian's parents' home, and I was interested to have seen the one of him on Aunt Helen's piano. When I asked Brian's mother about Malcolm and the reason for his death, she was cautious and told me very little.

'We never talk about it… something just went badly wrong,' was all I was told.

We lay by the river that afternoon, drinking in the early summer sunshine and loving the peace and calm of the water lapping at the bank. It seemed such a beautiful place to live; I looked back along the river to the far end of Elmwood's garden and marvelled at the house set in such a tranquil spot in the heart of busy London.

The house itself stood alone at the end of Gumber Lane, one of two large, impressive detached houses built at the turn of the nineteenth century, when all around had been fields and river land. More recently, newer houses had sprung up along the lane, but numbers one and three, which was Elmwood, remained separate and special. Each sat in its own large garden leading down at the back to the river, and separated from each other's land by a tall brick wall covered with ivy, and the wonderful honeysuckle. Tall elms grew around the garden, shading the banks of bluebells, and a pretty pond nestled at one side, where the cats basked and hoped for brave goldfish to swim up to the surface in error.

Inside Elmwood there were large, ornate drawing and dining rooms, their huge windows clad in thick velvet curtains, and their walls covered in heavy patterned paper, large mirrors and elaborate wall hangings. The deep carpets were rich in colour, and the ornaments and pictures depicted various places around the world that Uncle Tom had visited to lecture in physics.

At the side of the house was his study, the door of which was always closed. I later realised that I had never seen inside this room, and Brian thought it had always been kept locked.

There was a large kitchen, a breakfast room and a servants' room, with a bellboard from the days when the master and mistress of the house would ring for attention. The bellboard indicated which room the servant should go to, to receive orders. It all seemed very grand to me.

Two downstairs cloakrooms completed the ground floor, and there was a locked door to the basement cellar, used apparently for storage. On the first floor were four bedrooms, all with high ceilings, and all furnished with luxurious antiques and drapes. One bedroom was full of 'Malcolm'; clearly his old room and deliberately left in his memory. There were school photographs, bookshelves containing boys' annuals, encyclopaedias and academic books, and strangely, a large glass cabinet displaying dolls of all sizes from around the world. They wore national costumes from each of the different countries, and at a guess there must have been a good hundred dolls in all. This was Aunt Helen's collection, which she eventually promised to our daughter Lucy, who was the only girl in the family.

The first floor also had a small kitchen, converted for the use of Aunt Helen's mother, when she came to live with them as an elderly lady, until her death. Helen was an only child. There was a grand bathroom, a dressing room, a toilet and stairs to the attic floor which had of course originally been the servants' quarters. Lastly, up there in the attic was a small storage room leading to the loft space. No one in the family knew what was hidden in here, not for years and years, until it fell to us to clear the house when all of them had died.

Chapter Two

Over the following years we had intermittent contact with Uncle Tom and Aunt Helen. Special family occasions saw them present in the background, always together, always cool and a little distant. Uncle Tom had a warm and ready smile when we spoke, but if I watched him from a distance he looked sad.

When our first child was christened, my two old nursing friends joined us for the ceremony, and we all went home to lunch after church. Uncle Tom and Aunt Helen were with us as part of our family group, and Uncle Tom sat beside Mim (short for Miriam) for lunch. I remembered noticing how aloof he seemed to be when she was talking to him, and we mentioned it when she helped me to bring in the dessert after our first course of poached salmon, salad and new potatoes. It was the end of July, 1969, and a typically hot summer's day.

'Phew, Mags, this is hard going,' Mim said. 'Brian's uncle is a closed book, isn't he?'

She scraped the scraps from our plates into the rubbish bin under the sink for me, putting the used cutlery into a washing-up bowl.

'I mean, charming, of course,' she added awkwardly, 'but quite difficult to talk to.'

'Sorry, Mim. I thought you'd be just great with him; he's quite shy, I think.'

Rose joined us, carrying the salad bowls. It was so good to have them with us for Andrew's christening, and I always loved time spent with these two dear friends. We had lived together in a nurses' flat for the years before my wedding, and we felt totally at ease with one another.

Rose perched on the edge of the kitchen table, while I mixed in bananas to the bowl of fruit salad.

'What are you talking about?' she asked, noting our under-tones, and not wanting to miss any gossip.

'Nothing; honestly. Just Brian's uncle...'

'Hmm. He's quite mysterious, isn't he? I came back in their car—'

Mim was on the case as usual.

'Did you get anything out of him?' she asked at once. 'Conversation, I mean? I'm having quite a struggle, I can tell you;' she pulled a face...'but he really is charming,' she added hastily.

I took the pavlova from the tall, old fridge which almost filled the kitchen, but had so little space inside it.

'Probably you should just talk about physics or something,' Rose said, 'and he might open right up.'

Funny how I remembered that conversation particularly, later on.

It intrigued me that Aunt Helen wasn't at all close to my mother-in-law; there was certainly no animosity, but little affection between them either. And the two brothers had apparently always been close, as boys and as men, spending holiday time together in boats and enjoying a brotherly bond. Brian's mother was a true Yorkshire woman, given to pulling wonderful expressively blunt faces, which told of her opinion of a person or situation without any need for words. Many were the 'faces' we saw relating to Aunt Helen, though the two of them always maintained a familial warmth in our presence.

Our three children each received a card at Christmas containing a monetary gift from Tom and Helen, but the meetings between us all were rare. Excuses were always offered when we extended invitations to visit us in Ealing; we were told that the pressures of Uncle Tom's work at the Institute were great, they were otherwise engaged, or he was out of the country giving lectures.

Aunt Helen never came alone.

The years went by, and then, it seemed suddenly, Uncle Tom died of prostate cancer, untreated, when he was seventy-five.

Had we just not been aware of him, that we didn't know his health was declining? Weren't Brian's parents, or Auntie Pearl, his beloved sister, told that he was ill? Indeed, did even Aunt Helen know?

Shortly before he died, Uncle Tom came to Ealing as usual for *relating ? about ?*

his Christmas lunch. It was clear that he was unwell then, unable to eat as normal, pale, and clearly sitting in discomfort. Louise and I, both of us old nurses, questioned him gently but were politely rebuffed with the comment that he was 'seeing his doctor' about a minor problem after Christmas. For years Uncle Tom had come to Ted and Maud for lunch on Christmas day to be with the family, as Auntie Pearl always came to stay. She had been widowed young, her husband Cyril having died early from cancer, leaving her childless.

We all loved Auntie Pearl. She was a brave and jolly lady, always elegant, tall and graceful, and she loved all the children. My heart ached for her that she never had any of her own, for she needed so much care as her rheumatoid arthritis took hold and she became crippled in middle age. Despite this she was always bright and full of fun, and the children loved her.

Uncle Tom's condition was a shock to us all that Christmas.

'He looks awful, Brian,' I said, as we lay in bed on Christmas night. I warmed my cold feet against his hot ones and we ruminated on the day behind us; the pleasure of the time spent all together, and the joy on the children's faces as they opened new toys and presents. It was all, however, overshadowed by my concern for Uncle Tom.

Just a few months later he was dead. Clearly, the rapid decline in his health had taken him by surprise, and Aunt Helen told us he had died intestate, having never, she said, considered making a will. So unlike the astute man he had always been, was this the first sign that all had not been well for Uncle Tom for some time?

It was a shock for my father-in-law to be head of the family suddenly. Ted Fawley was the younger brother of the two, always, it seemed, in Tom's shadow since they were children. It was Tom who kept all the Fawley family treasures, the pictures, the silver, the photographs, indeed, all the mementoes. Tom to whom Pearl turned when she was widowed young, for advice and support, although Ted and Maud always loved her and welcomed her regularly into their home. And perhaps because of his academic brilliance and achievement and subsequently his knighthood too, Tom took the place of head of the family, leaving Ted always in second place.

lembranças

I loved my father-in-law, indeed, I loved both of Brian's parents. Maud was always the dominant one, Ted quietly gentle in the background; one could have thought submissive, but in truth he was often obstinate and firm. Never one to gossip, we heard extremely little from Ted about Tom's and Helen's marriage, and I wonder even now whether he knew what went on at all.

Tom Fawley's funeral in Barnes, in the beautiful old parish church near the river, was a big occasion in 1982. Dignitaries were there, representatives as you might expect from the Physical Science Institute, old Oxford University societies, and even the local Sea Scouts where Uncle Tom had a leading role before and after joining the RAF in the war. Many were the folk who came to pay their respects to a man loved and held in high regard in so many areas of society. We knew so little about him, really.

The coffin was covered with lilies. Early spring sunlight dappled through stained glass windows onto the flagstone floor, and picked out the long dark stamens of the big white flowers as the coffin was carried carefully up the aisle.

Behind it walked Aunt Helen of course; how, I thought she must have longed for son Malcolm's arm on which to lean. How she would have been remembering his funeral then; what pain she must have felt. Louise, beside me, pointed out a large ladder in one of Aunt Helen's stockings, so out of character for her, especially on important occasions such as this. She was dressed all in black, her cupid's bow lipstick slightly awry, and she was obviously struggling with the stress of the day. My heart ached for her.

But she didn't walk alone.

Right beside her, holding her up under one arm, for she was tiny and she looked like a frail little bird that day, was Gordon Lench, the neighbour from number one Gumber Lane, next door to Elmwood. A large man, over six foot tall, he wore a blank expression, but he showed gentle concern (out of character for him in general) for Aunt Helen.

'Why is he there, and not Dad?' I whispered to Brian, who shrugged, unperturbed.

'He's just being supportive, just a friend,' he muttered back. But I found it odd that within a warm and loving family such as ours this strange man who lived next door should take such an eminent place at Uncle Tom's funeral.

It was Gordon who read the eulogy during the service, apparently written, as well as delivered in full voice, by him. And yet we, the family, hardly knew this strange man.

Afterwards we went to Elmwood for tea. The fires were lit, despite early spring sunshine outside, for there was a chill in the air and the wind was strong in the elms and other trees in the garden. The river looked grey, and was flowing fast. I saw boys rowing by, training for events on the Thames in the summer ahead. There were no cats to be seen.

Perhaps fifty people came for tea, and left shaking Helen's hand, and assuring her of their high regard for Tom. No one mentioned Malcolm, whose funeral had taken place in the same church twenty-seven years before.

Throughout the afternoon, Gordon Lench stood beside Helen, puffing on his pipe. The air clouded around him, and my nostrils sensed the smell of his pipe smoke long after we had left the house.

Brian squeezed Aunt Helen's hand as we left...

'Just let us know if we can help you,' he said quietly. 'Anything we can do...'

She nodded.

'Thank you. I'll be all right, dear. But thank you.'

And Gordon stood right beside her, there in the doorway, as we walked down the drive to our car.

Chapter Three

'I'll phone Aunt Helen and ask her for tea,' I said, a couple of weeks later. 'She'll need us all right now; perhaps things have gone quiet, and she's all alone.'

'Fine, yes, good idea.'

Brian was mowing the lawn, giving it the first trim of the season, and he didn't stop to chat but turned and mowed the next row, keeping it straight until he reached the swing.

Cider our dog was stretched out in the sunshine on the patio, sleeping on a rug I had spread for his comfort on the flagstones. A feisty Welsh terrier, he had established his place in the family (at the top of course) from day one, when he came to us as a puppy of six weeks old.

Ours was an animal-orientated family, especially since James, at eleven years of age, had decided at that time, to become a vet on leaving school. It was not unusual for me to find him in the kitchen with a half-squashed hedgehog he had rescued from the road, attempting to bind its broken leg to a lollystick; or to discover a gruesome slow-worm he had found, being fed in one of my Tupperware boxes, surrounded by earth and stones.

On this occasion he was cleaning out the rabbit cages in the garden, and clean hay was blowing in the air from the large polythene sack he had torn open.

'James! What have you done with Rupert while you're doing that? Where is he?'

I was anxious lest the poor elderly rabbit had found its way in error into the dog, who was now sleeping off the heavy meal.

'He's in the lounge, Mum, don't panic,' came the reply.

Sure enough, Rupert the rabbit was comfortably sitting on the lounge carpet, having left a small pile of neat dry dropping pellets in the corner by the door. I sighed.

'I gave him some chickweed to keep him happy.' James continued with his cleaning duties, and I went inside to begin mine in the lounge.

I love sons.

Aunt Helen seemed delighted to be invited to tea, and having secured a day in a fortnight's time, I proceeded to sort out the travel details for her from Barnes to Ealing.

'Brian will fetch you in the car,' I volunteered.

'Well, thank you, Maggie... but to save him coming I'm sure Gordon would drive me over if he's free.'

I felt obliged to invite Gordon too.

'I'm sure he'd really love to come,' Aunt Helen said, sounding genuinely pleased I had asked him. 'He's a lonely man, you know, no one of his own.'

'Oh dear, why is that?'

'Well, once his wife died, many years ago, there was only Gordon and his son Paul, you see, and I can't say much for that relationship. Over the years they became estranged... he never has any contact with his son now, sadly.'

At first I was sorry for Gordon. It must be dreadful to be so alone in the world, and it seemed that he had no family, nor even close friends other than Helen and previously Tom. Together he and Helen became heavily involved in local wildlife schemes and formed a Wildlife Trust to protect threatened species or endangered birds. They organised trips to places of animal and bird interest, and raised money for a donkey sanctuary by holding garden parties at Elmwood in the summer months. In fact Helen in particular was well known in the area for her love of all birds and animals, and appeared in the local press when she established a special island on the reservoir to enable swans to nest safely without disturbance. I assumed that it was this mutual interest, and spare time on their hands, that brought the two of them together so often.

Gordon began to drive Aunt Helen to our house quite often to tea, sometimes just the two of them, sometimes with everyone for a family gathering, such as at Easter. Whenever Gordon came, his pipe came too, and shrouded the room in foul smelling smoke. He seemed pleased to be accepted and even sent boxes of chocolates at Christmas, but I personally, felt quite distinctly uncomfortable in his presence.

His one attribute was his gentleness to the children's pets, and even Cider warmed to him, which he never did to male strangers, or anyone who stood anywhere near his bed. Gordon was comfortable with animals, but clearly disliked people in general, especially women. I always felt uneasy with him, however hard I tried to be welcoming when he came.

These visits increased. Sometimes Aunt Helen came alone, when Brian would drive her in our car, but usually she was accompanied by Gordon, who gradually became more familiar. The children found him amusing, as it was all too easy to encourage him to get onto his high horse about some subject or another, and watch him lose his cool.

'You don't have to be in, Andrew, when Aunt Helen and Gordon come,' I suggested weakly one Saturday morning. 'I dare say there are other things you want to do.'

Andrew grinned mischievously. 'Not on your life, Mum,' he said. 'I wouldn't miss it for anything. We're planning to ask Gordon if he's watched *Dad's Army* this week.'

'*No*, Andrew, you really mustn't! You know how uptight he gets about comedy war-time programmes...'

'Precisely. Great for a laugh... we'll be careful.'

'But you never are, Andrew; you know how you wind him up! Last time it was after *'Allo 'allo* and you and James got him going about the French resistance. And then he always ends up saying how awful young people are!'

'Keep your hair on, Mum, we'll be the essence of respect. And Aunt Helen *loves* us...'

I had to smile because it was obviously true. As the years went by since Uncle Tom's death, Aunt Helen became warmer, and more fond of and interested in the children (and especially their pets) all the time. It was as if she felt sorry she had missed being a part of our family for so long, and now she was trying to make up for lost time.

Whenever she came, there were little gifts. A brooch or brace-let for Lucy, who loved pretty things; a book about rowing for James, who had started this sport at school, a couple of pounds for Andrew, and always marrowbone dog biscuits for Cider, bought specially when she discovered they were his favourite treat.

The children grew, alarmingly, into teenagers, and life for us, surrounding them, was ever fuller and busier.

One weekend, Brian and I drove to Elmwood to fetch Aunt Helen and take her to Kew Gardens. It was the end of the summer, and the lush foliage of the earlier months of June and July was losing its fresh green colour. The summer had been a hot one, and all around us as we strolled, the grass was thinning and pale in colour after the strong sun. Flowers were fewer, though still beautiful where they were regularly tended by a host of gardeners. We sat in the shade of a spreading oak tree, on a bench with a plaque bearing a dedication to Annette Morris – how pleasant to have a bench here in this tranquil place, in her memory.

Aunt Helen sat upright, as she always did, looking ill at ease, but obviously enjoying her afternoon out.

'Thank you both so much for bringing me here,' she said. 'It's a rare treat for me now. Tom and I used to come here sometimes, or Richmond Park, to walk and see the deer.'

'What's the event you've organised for next week?' Brian asked, aware that there was something grand arranged for the following Saturday at Elmwood.

'Oh, my garden party, you mean... for the Donkey Sanctuary. I'll be baking cakes and so on all week; there are lots of wildlife supporters coming, as well as the donkey people.'

We took Aunt Helen to the nearby teashop for afternoon tea and their famous Maids of Honour cakes, and then drove her back to Elmwood about seven o'clock. As we drove up to the end of the drive, Gordon was at the front door, as if waiting for Aunt Helen's return. It struck me as very strange to see him there, especially as she had been out. It was almost as though he had taken up residence at the house, and I felt once again that sense of foreboding and mystery that had gripped me before.

One weekend months later, an invitation arrived in the post. We were eating breakfast in the kitchen, warming ourselves with hot mugs of tea and watching snow falling in the garden through the window. Christmas preparations were under way.

'More cards; I heard the postman,' said Lucy, then aged fourteen. She went into the hall to collect the mail from the mat, and to retrieve some of it from Cider's teeth, as he objected violently to the intrusions through the letterbox. We had previously fitted a small cage to the door to collect letters as they arrived, in order to avoid chewed mail, but Cider, in true terrier form, was so annoyed by the contraption that he continued to leap at it when the post came. On one occasion he had to be lifted off the cage, having caught his teeth in the wire as he jumped, so the cage was removed and abandoned.

Lucy returned with a pile of Christmas cards and other envelopes, smeared with butter from her toast. She handed them around, the largest pile resting on my plate.

Sixteen-year-old James burst in as we opened envelopes, home from rowing training at school in Hammersmith.

'Hi... no one with you today then?' I enquired, secretly hoping that he was alone. My housekeeping budget was regularly down on Saturdays when the rowing crew joined us in urgent need of sustenance.

'No, just me. Any toast going?'

'James... put your kit in the washing machine, please, don't just drop it in the doorway. You look very muddy.'

'Shower in order, I'd say,' Brian commented hopefully.

'I've already had one at the boathouse. The mud is only on my stuff... we did a towpath run and it was knee-deep today where the snow's melted.'

James took two slices of bread from its wrapper in the bread-bin, and fed them into the toaster. I looked outside to see that pretty as the flakes were, falling softly and settling briefly on the branches, the grass looked wet and the pathway slushy. Not a white Christmas ahead then.

Andrew appeared at the bottom of the stairs. He had recently left the army, having joined the Royal Signals as a junior eight months ago, and he was catching up on lost sleep time at weekends by lying in late.

''S that you, James? I heard you leave at six-thirty this morning. Couldn't you go a bit more quietly?' He yawned and flicked the kettle on to make coffee.

A familiar pale green envelope sat in front of me amongst the pile, and I opened it, recognising Aunt Helen's tiny spidery writing on her personal writing paper.

'Oh, look what we have here!' I exclaimed, interested to see what the response would be. 'An invitation to Aunt Helen's eightieth birthday dinner! It's in four weeks' time, January twelfth at Elmwood. What do you all think?'

'That's nice.' Brian was usually positive.

'Do we all have to go?' Lucy pulled a face similar to one her grandmother could produce.

'Well, yes, I think we should. I expect the others will be going... Louise and David and the boys. And Grandma and Grandad, of course. Proper family occasion.'

'Not sure if I'll be free then...'

'James! It's a Sunday evening... you're bound to be free.'

The broad 'rowing' shoulders shrugged and he took another mouthful of toast. Andrew was usually compliant since joining the army, just glad to be home and with the family again. It appeared that his girlfriend Abby was invited too, so he was happy to join us. He went into the hall to phone her, with his coffee in one hand and several Christmas cards in the other.

'I think it will be fun.' I was trying hard to be encouraging, which is a major part of a mother's role and absolutely essential on these occasions. If Louise's two boys were going to the party I knew that our brood would enjoy the experience, albeit not really their sort of do. The five cousins were very close, living as they did within ten minutes' walk of one another, and having grown up so close in age. Peter was born in the year between Andrew and James, and Stuart only five weeks after Lucy. The cousins seemed more like brothers to our three, and they always enjoyed each other's company.

'Well, I think it will be grim,' said James with his mouth full. 'I'll only go if Pete and Stuart go.'

'I'll find out today. Louise will have had an invitation, I'm sure.'

Lucy, the only girl in our wide family, was typically herself.

'What will I *wear* Mum? Is it a grand do? Who else will be there?'

'Oh, no one, I expect, except the family. The invitation says 'family' dinner. So probably Auntie Pearl, and the rest of us, that's all. Your blue dress will be fine if it's evening dinner, and Aunt

Helen always does these things nicely. I'll probably wear my black dress with the flowers.'

'But my blue dress is old now, and too tight, I bet. Mum, I'll definitely need something new…'

Brian sighed and stood up to feed the dog, avoiding the clothes conversation, which always ended in another increase in the overdraft.

We all went to the dinner party.

Elmwood looked wonderful that night. As we drew up, with Brian's parents behind us in their car, we could see the lights of the house through the tall elms, and even a small Christmas tree sparkling merrily in the window.

My feet in their best patent strappy shoes slipped on the icy path, and my warm breath accompanied me in clouds. A glimmering frost had settled on the lawn, the trees and the garden bench near the door, looking like a delicate sifting of icing sugar on a cake. Aunt Helen was standing in the open doorway to welcome us all, looking very grand in a midnight blue lace dress and jacket.

'Wow, look at those earrings!' James whispered with a grin. Aunt Helen always wore impressively dangly things and tonight's were no exception. Diamonds twinkled, matching those in a pretty necklace, and on her fingers too.

'Hallo, hallo… come in, all of you!'

We all trooped inside, wiping our feet furiously to avoid marking the beautiful carpet with the grey, slushy ends of the January snow.

'Happy birthday!'

'Aunt Helen… happy birthday!'

'Helen dear, many happy returns.' That was my mother-in-law, joining us in the hall, carrying a large poinsettia in a pretty pot. Auntie Pearl followed her on Brian's arm and I noticed a visible decline in her walking. The arthritis was advancing. My father-in-law brought up the rear and closed the door behind him to keep out the winter chill. He stamped his feet on the mat and hung his overcoat on the large hallstand inside the porch.

Kisses from everyone for Aunt Helen, and presents, including our large bunch of flowers, for which she thanked us profusely.

Lucy preened herself in the oval carved giltwood mirror on the hall wall. Her new top and skirt, bought for Christmas and somewhat fashionably short, were a success.

Louise and David and the boys were late, and I smiled to myself as I thought of the struggle Louise was most probably having, in coaxing her teenage sons to come. We all trooped into the drawing room to await their arrival, and sat politely around the roaring log fire in the hearth. Somehow winter evenings at Elmwood were all the more opulent, with the long rich velvet curtains drawn against the cold, and the crackle of wood in the fireplace.

By now, there were apparently six cats. Only two, however, were in evidence, as being originally strays they tended to be shy of visitors and hid when anyone called.

The dinner was amazing. Aunt Helen had prepared it all herself, but there was a girl in the kitchen to help serve and later to clear up. Set out in the dining room was a whole poached salmon, with cucumber slices for eyes and a fan of dill for a tail.

'Do you have a fish kettle, Helen?' asked Auntie Pearl, needing help with the bones due to her severely arthritic fingers.

'Yes, oh yes, I have. And I do like to use it, because I do eat fish,' Helen explained, having become a firm vegetarian. She had also prepared meat, however, for the rest of us, and there were salads galore, potatoes and rice, and fascinating little eggs stuffed with a curry sauce.

'That was my first mistake,' muttered Brian's father quietly, passing his egg to one of the young ones who found it amusing. Not a curry man, Grandad.

Without exception, the family was there for Helen's eightieth party. I looked around at us all, enjoying the watching. A close-knit family, it was good to be part of something which revolved around Helen for a change.

There were roaring fires in the large dining room, the drawing room and the breakfast room, in front of which Plum and Benjy lay, curled up on a rag rug together, enjoying the warmth. Apparently Susie was hiding under Aunt Helen's bed, and the other three had disappeared altogether, to return once we had all left.

I noticed that the study door was closed as usual, and it also interested me that there was one person present who was not officially 'family'… Gordon, from next door, at 'number one'.

'Bit odd, don't you think?' I said to Brian later, as we lay in bed back at home. 'Why do you suppose Gordon was sitting at the head of the table?'

'Beats me, Mags. He's always around these days; I guess he's lonely too.'

'Well, I'm not surprised; he's a grumpy old chap… only nice to the cats. But why did he sit in what was always Uncle Tom's place? I just find it very odd.'

'Well, maybe he's just being supportive for Aunt Helen or something. He certainly hadn't a good word to say for young people today!'

We laughed as Brian mimicked Gordon's display during the evening of distaste towards the younger generation. Not at all a likeable man, I felt; a sentiment clearly shared by my mother-in-law.

'What's *he* doing here?' she had whispered to Louise and me as we helped serve the desserts. 'Goodness knows why Helen's invited him!'

I pulled the duvet over us to keep out the winter chill. The bedroom air was cold as our windows faced the open expanse of parkland opposite, and the icy wind howled through the trees outside. We cuddled close together; I always liked this time just before we slept, when we talked cosily about the day behind us. Tonight was somehow special, as we discussed the family and the evening spent all together.

'Your mother doesn't like Gordon much, and even Dad was noticeably polite towards him, rather than friendly,' I mused.

Brian huffed.

'Probably because of his pipe,' he said. 'Ghastly smell. He never stops puffing on that thing. I noticed a few weeks ago when I delivered the Christmas presents that Gordon's pipe was on the go then, and the whole house reeked of it.'

'Was he there then, as well? He must have been a great friend of Uncle Tom's to be there so much now… probably doing his duty in looking after Aunt Helen or something…'

'Oh no, I don't think so. Uncle Tom clearly found him an irritation I always fancied. I suspect it's Aunt Helen who's taken pity on him since he's all alone. And he does seem to share her love of cats and wildlife.'

We were all aware that increasingly, Aunt Helen's news involved local animals and birds that she had rescued, and that Gordon shared all these missions and activities with her. It was good to know that Aunt Helen was seemingly happy and coping with life without Uncle Tom, and we supposed her friendship with Gordon was partly responsible for this.

The phone was ringing one Sunday evening as we returned from church, and Brian raced inside to answer it, leaving me to lock the car. The children were all at home, busy doing different imperative things all over the house.

'Why doesn't anyone answer the *phone*?' shouted Brian, the front door wide open for all the street to hear. These were the days before the answerphone had arrived to grace our humble home and make life considerably easier.

'Oh hallo, Aunt Helen, good to hear you,' he was saying, calmly now, as I closed the front door. 'Yes, yes… I can do that. Certainly. How about Wednesday evening, I think that's free for me? Righto then, that'll be fine. Yes, yes I will. 'Bye now.'

I raised my eyebrows in question to him as he replaced the receiver.

'Aunt Helen wants me to go to Elmwood to talk business on Wednesday.' he said. 'Something to do with wills.'

'Well thank goodness for that,' I said, remembering that Uncle Tom had died without making one at all. 'That'll avoid a repeat situation, anyway. Wednesday evening's good… I'm going to Keep Fit with Joan.'

That Wednesday was a wet one, with rain lashing at the car windows as I drove to the church hall for our Keep Fit class. My friend Joan and I enjoyed a weekly session bending, stretching and generally giggling like teenagers at the sight of each other and ten other middle-aged women like ourselves, squeezed into an assortment of lycra fit to cause total insanity in any viewer. We were fewer that evening, probably because of the weather, and our class ended a little early.

'Where's Brian tonight?' Joan asked, as we changed out of our kit afterwards. 'I saw his car was missing as I drove past your house.'

'He's over at Elmwood tonight, talking wills with Aunt Helen, as he's her executor. I think she's using a solicitor in Sheen who is an old friend too, but quite a bit younger, apparently.'

Joan's eyebrows shot up.

'Hey, that's good news. Maybe you'll be set to inherit a fortune...'

'Oh, wouldn't that be great? Somehow I doubt it though, knowing our luck in general.' I struggled with a knot in the lace of one trainer. 'There certainly ought to be a fair whack for somebody one day, but I honestly doubt it will be us.'

As my Keep Fit kit was circling in the washing machine at half past ten, I wondered what was taking Brian so long in Barnes. He came in with the usual whistle for Cider, as I was sponging something sticky from the kitchen table, remnants from Lucy's supper, which she had cooked for us earlier.

Brian planted a kiss on my cheek as I switched on the kettle for the third time.

'You've been hours,' I commented. 'Everything OK?'

He smiled and raised his eyebrows positively.

'Better than OK, actually. Pretty good, I'd say. Aunt Helen ran through her will with me, and it's more or less ready to be drawn up with the solicitors now.'

I spooned coffee into the cafetière.

'Well? You look rather chuffed.' I thought of my conversation earlier with Joan.

Brian dug around in the biscuit tin for his favourite digestives, and grinned.

'The will's a bit bizarre to say the least,' he said, 'but Louise and I stand to inherit a fair old sum each one of these days. We're the only relatives of our generation that Aunt Helen's got. She wants you and Louise to go for coffee one morning and make lists of furniture that you'd like...'

'Wonderful! Those antiques!'

'Well, I don't know what you've got in mind doing with them. Everything's much too big and old-fashioned for our house.'

'Brian! What about that gorgeous blue velvet loveseat? And the Fawley clock? You couldn't let them go! Not to mention some of those lovely little tables, all inlaid and polished…'

My mind skipped on ahead, picturing with delight the beautiful pieces of furniture I had loved since I first saw them years before. The visit with Louise was arranged.

My sister-in-law, seven years my senior and also an ex-nurse, co-incidentally from the same London hospital as myself, had become a good friend. We lived close by and often looked after each other's children, as well as sharing family meals and belonging to the same church. As a non-driver, she had to agree to be driven by me to Elmwood in time for coffee. When we arrived, Aunt Helen's handyman was busy in the garden; sadly, it seemed, digging a small grave under a shady tree. We all exchanged hugs as Aunt Helen told us how her beloved Susie had died in the night.

'I found her cold and still beside me on the bed when I woke,' she said. There were tears in her eyes which spilled slowly down one cheek and onto her jumper as she spoke. 'Just lying there… so peaceful really, but already gone.'

Together we wrapped Susie's still little body in some old flannelette sheeting; 'Warm for her,' Helen commented childishly, but I understood so well. The death of a much-loved pet is always hard to bear, and poor Helen had coped with so much death already.

We laid Susie in the shallow grave dug in the side garden in the shade of the woodland area, where bluebells appeared so suddenly and mysteriously every spring. Louise and I watched as Aunt Helen threw some soil over the little flannelette bundle, and then we led her indoors, leaving Fred the handyman to finish the job.

Our coffee was already laid on the breakfast room table, not, we noticed, as elegantly as normal.

'I'm not myself today,' Aunt Helen sighed sadly. 'I'll miss little Susie so badly. I've just put our coffee ready in here, if you girls don't mind… you pour for me Louise, would you, dear?'

She almost slumped in one of the comfy chairs, normally used by a cat. Aunt Helen never slumped; such an erect and elegant lady, who always preferred an upright chair and never appeared to relax. My heart went out to her, as I remembered the death of my own pets years ago, and how heartbroken I had been.

The door to the garden was thrown open, and Gordon Lench appeared, carrying a small wooden cross.

'Ah… hallo, hallo. Louise, Maggie. You'll have heard the news.'

We nodded.

'Yes indeed. So sorry.'

'Hallo, Gordon, what have you got there?' Aunt Helen fetched a fourth cup from the china cupboard (no mugs in this house) as he showed her the cross.

'I've done this for you,' he said. 'Tell me what you'd like written on it, and I'll paint it on.'

Louise and I later commented to one another that it seemed strange when Gordon came in through the kitchen door, and not via the front door, coming as he was, from 'number one' along the lane. We did not then know that a secret route had long since been erected between the two houses; a ladder was placed up the wall on one side, and another down on the other side, at the far end of the adjoining gardens, and hidden in the tall shrubbery. Aunt Helen later explained that this was to maintain privacy from the neighbours along the lane; she thought it would be unseemly and frowned upon if Gordon was seen calling on her too frequently, and in fact he called several times a day.

The little cross was painted with the words: 'SUSIE' and the date, followed by 'Loved and loving to the end.'

When we left at lunchtime it was drying in the sun, and later placed over the grave, where it remains to this day.

Aunt Helen took Louise and I through each room in the house to choose our antiques for the list. There were so many beautiful things, and she said it gave her pleasure to know that one day we would look after them all and keep them in the family, to pass on eventually to our children. We admired the two grandfather clocks in the downstairs reception rooms, and Aunt Helen explained that the wonderful eighteenth-century one in the dining room was the Fawley family clock, to be left to Brian, and the other in the drawing room, was her own old family one for Louise.

'Look, I've written notes to put inside each one,' she said, 'because if there should ever be any mistake in the future, that will explain my wishes.'

Sure enough, handwritten slips of paper stating 'For my nephew, Brian Fawley.' And 'For my niece, Louise Easby' were secured by sellotape inside each pendulum case.

Aunt Helen marched us up to the first floor of the house, to show us the glass cabinet full of foreign dolls. 'Now then, Maggie, these are for Lucy,' she said. 'As the only girl amongst all your children, I think she should have my collection one day.'

I thanked Aunt Helen, and noticed another little note naming Lucy, taped inside the cabinet.

Each of our boys was allocated a certain treasure, and we could tell that much consideration had taken place, and much pleasure gained in the planning of these gifts. All, of course, to be distributed when Aunt Helen herself was 'no more'. We had become really fond of her in recent years, and I found myself hoping that such a time would prove to be a long way ahead.

The surprising thing was the rest of the will. Brian had seen what had been drawn up of course, and had told me of Aunt Helen's wishes. The wonderful old house…'Elmwood'… was to be left to the Cats' Charity, with specific instructions that rather than being sold, it should be turned into a cats' home for strays, with a resident veterinary surgeon who would treat and care for them. His salary was to be paid from the balance of the estate after family members had received their individual bequests. A substantial sum of money was to be left to both Ted and Pearl, Helen's brother-in-law and sister-in-law, and a smaller sum, together with the chosen furniture, for both Brian and Louise. No one else was mentioned in the will at all.

We were not, as a family, surprised about these wishes, given that in recent years Aunt Helen had become increasingly strange in her obsessive behaviour towards her cats. She had arranged for cat shelters to be built in one corner of the garden for strays, which were carpeted for their comfort and warmed in cold weather. At times there were no fewer than ten cats in the house, and others, which were really wild creatures, adopted the shelters as their homes in the garden. The beautiful garden, which Uncle Tom had tended so lovingly was littered with dishes of cat food and bowls of milk and water. Elmwood began to smell inside when we visited.

'I don't know which I like less; the pong of cat pee or Gordon's filthy old pipe,' Brian mused. 'Things aren't like they used to be, when Uncle Tom was alive.'

Indeed, things were not.

Chapter Four

I used to wake in the night, worrying about my children. Sometimes, if a fearful dream had woken me, I would leave the bed
carefully so as not to disturb Brian, and pad softly in my slippers
downstairs to the kitchen, to make tea and ease my troubled
mind. Sometimes I would lie quite still, hoping to slide back into
sleep; and I listened for cars to count as they passed our gate on
their way into the night.

Often I woke around 3 a.m. in those still hours before dawn,
when all the house was sleeping. Outside I could see the orange
glow of the street lamp just beside our gate, and in summer I
listened for early birdsong as the little creatures woke in the park
trees opposite our house. Occasionally I leant on the windowsill
in the stillness, just watching the night. Sometimes a lone fox
prowled along, searching for rubbish sacks to investigate on his
hunt for food. Night-times were usually peaceful.

Beside me, Brian lay sleeping soundly, always. He was a loud
sleeper; sometimes muttering, often snoring in the deep thickness
of sleep. If I reached out I could feel his warm back hunched
under the duvet, and it gave me a gentle reassurance. His hair had
thinned on top with the passing years, but there were new tufts
on his shoulders and chest, as though the hair had forgotten
where it was really meant to grow. His waist had thickened,
though not as much as mine, and his face had become slacker. He
looked very serious when he slept, and often I noticed new
anxiety lines and furrows creasing as he mumbled in a dream.

James was at university now; Lucy about to go, and Andrew
was living with four friends in a flat nearby, and working in
London. How quickly the years sped by.

One of our pleasures as a family over recent years had been
following James's rowing career. A competent rower at school, he
progressed to the British national crew and rowed abroad and at
home, proudly wearing the England strip. At university he was

studying Sports Science for his degree, and rowed in events most weekends and trained every day. In order to train for the GB crew he had to have his own scull and blades, made to measure for him in Finland. Aunt Helen, always a keen follower of the Boat Race in Barnes, was delighted to hear of James's success, and even came with us on occasions around London, to watch the regattas in which he took part. She kindly wrote a cheque when the Finnish boat and blades were delivered from abroad, and wanted news of every event as it took place thereafter.

There had been a couple of girlfriends while James was still at school, but they soon tired of standing on a towpath, holding James's empty Wellington boots while he trained. It was indeed a surprise to us all when he met Lesley at university and fell deeply in love, and they became engaged when he was only twenty-one. That same year, when James was training daily, he began to experience severe back pain, and was warned by the team physiotherapist that all was not well with his spine.

No wonder I worried... what son ever listens to his mother... James was intent on his training and we could tell his dream was to be chosen to row in the Olympics one day. He continued to row.

Just before his final exams he came home one weekend with Lesley. I watched them together, and delighted in their love.

On the Saturday evening we were to have supper in the garden. Early summer had brought evening sunshine onto our patio, and I carried a tray of cutlery out to lay the table while the chops sizzled on the barbecue.

'Maggie, let me help,' Lesley offered, uncurling herself from the sunlounger on the lawn. A pretty girl, also a sports scientist, she had completed her degree the year before James and was currently finishing her post-graduate certificate in education to enable her to teach.

Her dark hair hung thick and shiny to her shoulders, and her deep brown eyes sparkled with the thrill of wedding plans and happy thoughts of the future with James.

'Lovely; thank you. I'll get the glasses and plates. How's the meat doing, James?'

He stood tall and strong by the barbecue, tongs in hand, tanned already in late May, from so much time on the river in all weathers.

'Almost ready. Unless you want it burnt.' That ready smile, vibrant blue eyes like his father. They made a handsome couple, I thought proudly.

We ate our meal and sat late on the patio, hearing and sharing wedding plans for a year's time.

Only a matter of weeks later, Brian drove to fetch James from university as the year ended and finals were done. They strapped his rowing scull onto the roof of our long estate car as they had done between them, every time the holidays had begun or ended for the past three years, and set off home along the motorway to London.

We shall never understand what happened, but suddenly the wind caught the boat in the outside motorway lane and sent it crashing into the central reservation, causing dramatic damage, but most thankfully of all, no accident to cars or people on the road at that time.

Our telephone rang that afternoon, and it was Brian on his mobile phone, his voice sounding shaky.

'Mags… we'll be late. Had a spot of bother on the M6. We're on the hard shoulder now, waiting for recovery…'

'What? Why? Oh, God, what's happened?' my mind was running ahead and filling itself with terrifying thoughts.

'Darling, it's OK, we're both all right. We've had an accident with the boat and it just flew off the roof and settled in the central reservation. Now we're waiting for a pick-up for it and we may be some hours before we can sort this out and get home.'

'Is James all right?'

'Yes, yes, we're both fine, no one hurt. Just shaken. And the boat's a mess…'

Little did we realise then that the loss of the boat while it was being repaired was a blessing in disguise. Missing daily training brought out the hidden back pain that James had been aware of at a minor level, and the problem became acute. After much specialist investigation and advice, he had to give up competitive rowing, and opt for a coaching role.

Lesley was a huge support and help, and planning for their wedding also helped to lessen the disappointment for James. I was just relieved that more serious damage had not been done, and indeed thankful that he was not confined to a wheelchair for the rest of his life.

The wedding was fantastic, on the hottest day of the year, and set in a spot in Burton-on-Trent that was picture postcard material.

James looked stunning in his navy morning suit, every inch the handsome bridegroom. Andrew, as best man, also filled the bill and made a splendid speech as well. Lucy read the lesson in church in lieu of being a bridesmaid, and Lesley looked just beautiful.

'Haven't we just had the most wonderful day?' I mused afterwards, kicking off my wedding outfit shoes in our hotel bedroom. Brian, still grinning like the proud father he always was, kissed my neck.

'Wonderful,' he said.

'And everyone was here. Except my Dad. How thrilled he would have been with it all.' I peeled off my lilac dress and hung it on the padded hanger on the wardrobe door.

'He would indeed,' Brian agreed thoughtfully. 'But we'd all have been so anxious about him if he'd been here, Mags. Too much for him... far too much. Just as well, really, although we missed him.'

My father, ever the most loving, adoring Grandpa to our children, had died nine months before, having struggled for years with respiratory problems which finally resulted in heart failure. We all missed him so much, and never more than at family occasions when he had always held central place. I thought of him now, as I brushed my hair, newly coloured a light golden brown to hide the grey streaks, and just remembered him with love.

'I know, Bri. I know you're right, but somehow I still want him here with us all. Even if he'd had to have his oxygen, and there'd have been all those problems... I just *want* him still.' Brian stood behind me and hugged me close. I took such comfort from the warmth and proximity of him; we needed no words. Following Dad's death, my mother came to live with us, elderly, an invalid for years, and needing so much care. She missed Dad dreadfully, and died fourteen months later, unable to live without him.

We were increasingly aware that whenever we visited Elmwood, Gordon was there with Aunt Helen. Whenever we made arrangements for her to visit us, he came too. In fact it seemed that they were seldom apart at all. Ted and Maud, Brian's parents, never pretended to like Gordon, and indeed, I too often said that I found him an unpleasant man who left me feeling uncomfortable in his presence. He was prone to unnecessary outbursts of temper, and was always appallingly critical.

He appeared to have no friends, other than Wallace Beasby of Beasby and Green, solicitors in Barnes. Wallace and Gordon had played and watched cricket together years before, when Gordon had first been married and moved to 'number one' Gumber Lane. It was Wallace who arranged for Gordon and his wife Florence to purchase the house in 1955, having been renting it originally from an old colonel who owned the house but lived in another, in Knightsbridge, himself.

I remember one weekend over tea, Aunt Helen made a some-what critical joke about Wallace, and received a vehemently angry response from Gordon.

'Well,' she argued quietly, 'I certainly know I shouldn't ask Wallace to deal with anything on my behalf... I just don't think he's trustworthy. That's why I've dealt with Will Rogers in Sheen over my will. You liked him, didn't you, Brian?'

'Yes, yes I did. Seems a good fellow I should say.'

Gordon was muttering as he puffed, causing an extra waft of pipe smoke to hang in the air. I made a mental note to open all windows as soon as they left.

Shortly after this visit I heard from Aunt Helen on the phone that she had been to see the doctor, and he had diagnosed asthma. Not helped, I felt quite certain, by the constant fug she was forced to breathe in Gordon's company.

We watched her health deteriorate, and sadly the day came when we realised that she was seriously ill.

Brian had been to Elmwood one Sunday after lunch to run through some papers with Aunt Helen which she had found confusing. As he was about to leave for Barnes, I pulled on my jacket and decided to go too.

'I'd like to see Aunt Helen,' I said, feeling a twinge of unpro-voked concern. 'I just feel I want to come.'

'Yes, why not? I'd like your company in the car anyway.' Brian snapped the catch on his briefcase, an old one now marked 'Aunt Helen' on a yellow sticker on its front. 'But it may be a bit boring when I'm going through the business stuff with her.'

'There's always Gordon,' I grinned. 'But don't leave us alone together too long... I might be overcome with unbridled passion!'

'I'll take that as a serious threat then, shall I?'

I loved Brian's mischievous smile.

The house was in a sad state that afternoon. Aunt Helen, then eighty-eight, looked frail and ill, and there were food stains on her dress, something I had never seen before. The smell of cats was stronger than ever, and the thick pile carpets covered in moulted fur.

'My cleaning girl has given up,' Aunt Helen told us. 'I'm sorry everywhere is in such a dreadful mess.'

I gave her a gentle hug, feeling sad at the loss of her dignity. For one so genteel, she appeared pitiful, and my heart was heavy.

'Don't you worry,' I said quietly. 'Now, how about letting me do a bit for you as I'm here? I'd really like to help.'

'No, no, certainly not Maggie, thank you.' She struggled with a bout of coughing. 'It's this asthma; it just exhausts me. Polly gave up last week... said she couldn't clean here any more because of the cats.'

'Well let me help you while I'm here,' I urged, looking around at the potential squalor of the once beautiful drawing room. A cat pooh was winking at me on the fender, and the stench in the room hung heavily around us, a mixture of cat excrement and stale tobacco.

'Maggie's great with a hoover,' encouraged Brian. 'And she's never happier than when she's washing up.'

I gave him a mean look, unseen by Aunt Helen. She shrugged, too exhausted to argue, and I went into the kitchen to make myself useful while the two of them talked business.

I was shocked by what I found. The breakfast room was disgusting, inhabited as it clearly was, by a number of mangy strays which were obviously not housetrained. The stench was overpowering.

In the kitchen, used utensils were piled in the sink unwashed.

Bowls of cat food and milk, however, appeared fresh and clean. Aunt Helen cared for her cats before herself, it was clear.

I ran a finger along a ledge and then wished I hadn't. Surface cleaning had not taken place in here for some while, and this was a food preparation area. I was increasingly concerned. Anyone with very little knowledge would surely be aware of the dangers of such poor hygiene, especially in a kitchen. I thought of the disease toxoplasmosis, which was a real threat where these cats were wandering freely amongst food and work surfaces.

A rather fearful black moggie pushed his face through the cat flap and on seeing me, a stranger, backed out again hastily. At least, I felt, with all these cats around, it should keep rats and mice away. Otherwise, they would have a field day in this kitchen.

In trepidation, I opened the walk-in pantry door and peered inside. What confronted me left me aghast.

Tinned food lined the shelves, safe, I supposed in the sealed cans. Bottles, however, looked dubious, some having been opened, it would seem, a long time ago. Orange squash was an unnaturally dark colour, with a thick grey sediment at the bottom. I made a mental note to avoid asking for a cold drink during any future visits. A blue and grey mould lined the sides of an open jar of strawberry jam.

I looked tentatively into a cake tin and was horrified to find the remains of an old sponge cake, covered in green fur.

I foraged in the cupboard under the sink and found a plastic dustbin sack, into which I set to work to clear the offending articles at once. As I went back into the pantry, I discovered a pile of old woollies on the floor under the far shelving; jumpers and warm clothes which had obviously made a cosy bed on which a cat could have her kittens.

I worked hard in the kitchen, clearing and wiping, washing sticky chutney rings on shelves, cleaning pots and pans and crockery in the sink, until Brian called me from the hallway ages later.

'Mags! Where are you? What're you doing?'

I hastily dried my hands on the towel around my waist in lieu of an apron, and called back:

'I'm here! Just finishing the kitchen.'

He appeared in the doorway, wrinkling his nose at the cat smell.

'Phew! Bit much, eh?'

'I've been holding my breath,' I whispered. 'But that's not the worst of it. Herewith one sack of horrors from hell.' I indicated the rubbish I had cleared, now well tied with string and ready for hasty disposal. Brian took it outside to the dustbin to await the weekly collection. He returned feigning nausea, fortunately not observed by Aunt Helen, who had arrived in the kitchen to find me.

'Maggie dear, you're a marvel. Thank you so much… I'm really ashamed of all this.'

I gave her a gentle hug.

'Nothing to be ashamed of,' I tried reassuringly. 'I've just done a bit of clearing up; kept me busy and entertained while you two were doing the necessary. Shall I make us some tea? The kettle's boiled.'

Several times over, I didn't add, to give me boiling water for my chores. I felt certain that poor Aunt Helen was unaware of the horrors of her pantry shelves; she looked so tired and I suspected that it was some time since she had made a decent meal for herself. I couldn't remember her ever allowing me to make tea or coffee in her kitchen before, but this time she nodded gratefully, which seemed to set off more rasping coughs.

We returned to the drawing room with the tea tray and were joined by several different cats. Aunt Helen named them all, stroking and petting them lovingly, her expression suddenly one of pleasure and contentment.

'Look at Sophie here, isn't she just beautiful? When she came she was so matted and dirty, her fur full of lumps and burrs from the wasteland where she was found. I've spent so many hours gently brushing her, but she won't allow anyone else near.'

Sophie was a long-haired Persian cat, eyeing Brian and me suspiciously, as she purred on Aunt Helen's lap. Beside her on the blue chaise longue were two others; a tabby looking overfed and elderly, and a sprightly little black cat, which played with the fringe on the seat.

'This is Coco, Gordon's cat,' Aunt Helen explained with a smile.' She seems to have taken up residence with me lately. She's so friendly and sweet.'

At which, we heard heavy footsteps in the hall, and Gordon appeared around the door, an extra cup in hand.

'I saw you all through the window,' he announced, pouring himself the last of the tea in the pot. I glanced at Brian... Gordon had obviously come over the wall via the ladder to have passed this rear window. We were careful not to smile.

'Brian's been running through a few things with me,' Aunt Helen explained. 'And Maggie's done stalwart work in the kitchen.'

Gordon gave me half a look of acknowledgement.

'I did notice that the washing up was done,' he said.

Hmph, I thought to myself. Pity you didn't do it first.

He began to stuff his pipe with his evil-smelling tobacco from a tin in his jacket pocket. As he lit it and puffed repeatedly to get it to ignite, Aunt Helen's coughing began again. Brian looked annoyed.

'I don't think your pipe smoke's helpful, you know, Gordon,' he said anxiously. 'This cough is much worse, I'm sure. What does the doctor say?'

Aunt Helen was unable to answer, her face in what I noticed was a less than clean large handkerchief.

Gordon shrugged, looking somewhat aggressive, and more than a little guilty.

'Doctor! What doctor?' he huffed. 'The man's a quack, that's for sure! Quite useless. We're not bothering with him.'

'He wanted me to have tests at the hospital,' Aunt Helen said, having temporarily recovered. 'but Gordon thinks it's a waste of time. Just asthma, after all.'

Brian was indignant. 'Well, I'm not so sure,' he said. 'I think you must do what the doc. advises. You may need something extra for that cough.'

Despite our pleas and regular encouragement, no tests were undertaken for several months.

I was talking to Auntie Pearl on the telephone one morning; our regular routine call to check on her since she had become more crippled and disabled with arthritis. Her sight was very limited now, but fortunately she lived in an excellent flat in a block with a resident warden in Merton Park.

Auntie Pearl was a family favourite, loved dearly by us all, and admired for her courage. Her sense of humour was a particular asset, and I could hear the smile in her voice over the phone.

'That Gordon needs fumigation,' she said. 'His dreadful pipe... no wonder Helen's choking is so bad. Why on earth doesn't she *tell* him, I wonder?'

'It's much worse now. You haven't seen her for months, have you, not since you all came to us at Easter?'

'Well, I've spoken on the phone, and the poor dear coughs all the time. I'd like to get my hands round Gordon's throat, I can tell you.'

'You should see the house, Auntie Pearl. It's so sad. Such a mess, and a frightful smell of cats. There are extras now I'm sure, and Brian says there are more living in the shelters in the garden, too.'

'Pity Gordon's not in one of those. Best place for him... and his pipe. Is he ever in his own house these days? Whenever I phone Helen he's there with her it seems.'

In the early days of their marriage, Auntie Pearl and her long-dead husband Cyril had lived at Elmwood with Tom and Helen. She often told us of those happy times, and shared occasional memories of Malcolm as a small boy, something never mentioned by other members of the family. Pearl and Helen had formed a friendship certainly beyond the bounds of sisters-in-law, and indeed now, in their latter years, Helen supported Pearl financially in no small way, ensuring her the little extra comforts that her illness required.

'Auntie Pearl, I'm coming over on Thursday with Louise. Do you remember we fixed Thursday? Is that still OK? We'll bring those photos that we wanted to show you, and the shoes I bought for you to try.'

'Thursday will be fine, dear, I'm looking forward to it. I wish I could say come to lunch...'

'No, no... no need at all. We'll make a pot of tea when we come, perhaps. Don't bother making any of your buns though, I'll bring some.'

Visual limitations meant that Auntie Pearl now threw in a handful of this and that for her baking, unable to check scales or packets for amounts. Her sultana buns were somewhat hit and miss, and probably best avoided.

Louise and I had chosen a wet afternoon on Thursday, and the drive to Merton Park was mildly hazardous. As usual, of course, I drove, and my passenger, normally nervous in the car, was not at her best.

'Good Lord, I'm relieved we're here,' she mumbled, stepping out of the passenger door into a large puddle. 'I feel quite sick.'

Not a good traveller, Louise.

Auntie Pearl was at the window, two floors up, but I couldn't tell whether she could see us parking below. We used the lift inside, which was equipped with a red emergency cord for elderly residents, and a chair on which to perch. Louise settled herself on it, still recovering from my driving.

'She's seen us... the door's open.'

We walked from lift to flat along the wide corridor, cheerfully decorated with fresh flowers on the wide low windowsill. 'Hallo, my dears, come on in.' Auntie Pearl welcomed us from the small sitting room, where she was seated in her specialist chair, known to the family as her ejector seat.

We all exchanged hugs, and Louise and I selected the cleanest chairs on which to sit, first removing the small bits of food debris that had escaped notice.

Pearl and Cyril Legget had never been blessed with children. He had been a tailor in Wimbledon, a friendly, rotund, good-looking man, always well turned out. They made a striking couple when young; she, elegant and beautiful, always upright and slightly taller than Cyril, and he immaculate and jolly. Strange how life goes really, I thought... now Pearl was bent and crippled, and Cyril had died at fifty-five of stomach cancer.

I never remember Auntie Pearl complaining. Always one to make the best of things, she seldom ever told her family how difficult her daily struggle had become. She maintained her dignity and interest in us all throughout her life, and was consequently much loved.

Louise made the tea and I unpacked provisions; a jam sponge made that morning, a couple of portions of casseroles sufficient for one, and a small chicken pie, to go into the little fridge.

'Auntie Pearl, there's some beef stew here for your lunch tomorrow. And a little of our lamb casserole, with all the vegetables in it. Easy to warm up.'

'Thank you Maggie. Lovely. I'll enjoy that… what would I ever do without you two girls? I've been thinking, you know, about taking Meals on Wheels…'

'Super idea. That would really be a help.'

Louise poured tea in three mugs.

'But I'm not sure I'd like what they'd provide you know… not so good as what you bring me, that's for sure.'

'It depends which of us has been cooking,' I suggested, knowing Louise's offerings were far more palatable than mine. Pearl, however, was always grateful and scraped all our dishes clean.

She smoothed her skirt over her knees and crumbs from lunch flew onto the carpet. A Polish girl called Eva came twice a week to clean and shop and keep the flat tidy and presentable, but inevitably, given Pearl's condition, there were mishaps and accidents between visits. Increasingly, Louise and I were aware of the need for more care for Pearl, but finance was a problem and she clearly wanted to remain in her home for as long as possible. Thank heavens for Aunt Helen's monthly contribution, which enabled Pearl to buy her 'ejector seat' and other aids to normal living which were becoming essential rather than just helpful now. I was glad that Lucy, now living not far from Auntie Pearl in a flat with other physiotherapist friends, often came to visit in her spare time, and was able to bring shopping and do odd personal jobs for her. The relationship between the two of them was a special one, and I knew that they loved each other dearly.

We sipped our tea and Louise and I produced family photographs of recent events. Pearl showed much interest, but was hardly able to tell who was who in the pictures with her failing eyesight.

'I'm sure my sight is getting worse,' she said. 'Does the flat look dusty to you? I really can't see it but I think Eva cleans pretty well for me.'

There was toothpaste, I thought, on Pearl's jumper, but I didn't point it out.

'Everything's spot on, Auntie Pearl. Lovely and clean.'

'I spoke to Gordon, you know, on the phone this week. I'm really very worried about Helen... he said she wasn't well enough to talk to me. Coughing dreadfully, he said. Have either of you seen her?'

Louise hadn't, but I told them both of our recent visit, and how Brian and I had both been concerned. I lightened the tale considerably, however, so as not to worry Auntie Pearl. On the way home in the car, Louise brought the point up again.

'Maggie, I'm worried about Aunt Helen,' she said, as we drove through Richmond Park in the rain. The windscreen wipers were working hard against the torrential downpour, and no deer were to be seen at all in the parkland.

'You said things were bad when you went over.'

'I should say so. The state of the place is horrendous... when you think what Elmwood used to be like, and now it's really in decline.'

I told Louise about the kitchen, and my efforts at cleaning and clearing away rotten food.

'And Aunt Helen looked really awful. Frail and exhausted, with a hacking cough. She was resisting any tests though... the doctor has suggested some.'

'Why won't she go, for heaven's sake?'

'Oh, Brian thinks she doesn't want to be told to leave Elmwood. In case they want to hospitalise her, or something. Who'd look after the cats, and so forth, you know what she's like. And anyway, Gordon is quite adamant that the doctor is useless. A quack, he called him.'

'He's a real pain, that man... Gordon, I mean, not the doctor. What's it to do with him anyway? I reckon he's partly responsible if he's still smoking that dreadful pipe all the time!'

'Oh, he certainly is! It's like a fog that smells of burning socks; makes me choke, let alone Aunt Helen. Brian reckons he's there all the time you know, virtually living there these days. Did you notice Auntie Pearl said he answered the phone and didn't let Aunt Helen speak to her?'

'I did, yes, and I thought that was odd. We'd better check on Aunt Helen... I'll phone tonight.'

I was aware by the speedometer that I had stepped somewhat too vigorously on the accelerator in my annoyance with Gordon as we spoke. Slowing gently, I thought of the effect the wretched man was having on us all in one way or another, and yet we were all mystified as to his intentions where Aunt Helen was concerned. If, as a friend, he was anxious about her, surely he would be encouraging her to follow the doctor's instructions? What was in his mind, I wondered, to behave as he did?

It transpired that each time we telephoned after this, Gordon took the call and refused to allow any of us to speak to Aunt Helen, because, he said, it would aggravate her cough.

We visited more often as a result, and were met with increasing rebuff on Gordon's part. One evening after work, Brian drove to Barnes with documents to be signed, and was shocked at what he found.

Elmwood was barely lit, and the downstairs windows dark and unwelcoming from the drive. It was early November, and the evening was gloomy, seemingly dark earlier than usual that day in the late afternoon. Gordon opened the door to Brian and invited him into the dining room.

'Helen's not well tonight,' he sighed, exhaling stale smelling tobacco smoke. He was prone to sighing, usually as a sign of irritation, and his general air was unwelcoming and indeed, Brian felt, distinctly unfriendly.

'I've sent her to bed early. You could leave this stuff with me, and I'll get her to sign it in the morning.'

Brian noticed that although it was only eight thirty, Gordon was wearing his dressing gown.

'Looks like it's early bed all round,' he commented.

'Yes, well... I'm living here now, you know. I've moved my things into the back bedroom so as to look after Helen. She needs help in the night now; can't be left alone, you see.'

'Oh dear, Gordon... why weren't we told? I'd no idea she was this ill, really. What does the doctor say?'

Brian laid the documents on the once-beautiful walnut dining table, which had not seen polish for many months. He could hear Aunt Helen coughing upstairs, and was very worried, but Gordon's response was angry and far from encouraging.

'Hmph! Don't mention that fellow to me!' he almost shouted. 'We'll have no doctors here! The idiot is insisting on hospital tests and I've already put my foot down as you know, but Helen has agreed to go against my wishes! Ridiculous... I can look after her perfectly well, you know, we don't want anyone's help here!' Calmly, Brian enquired further about the 'tests' and discovered that a special X-ray amongst other explorations was booked for later in the week. As a family we were shocked and saddened to learn later that the results of these proved Aunt Helen to be suffering from tuberculosis. She did, however, refuse treatment in hospital, and determined to stay at home with her beloved cats for comfort, and Gordon as her resident nurse and carer. Not a reassurance for us as a family in any way, but of course we had to abide by her wishes. The knowledge that Gordon was in sole command at Elmwood only aggravated our concern, which continued to increase dramatically over the following months.

Chapter Five

'Mum, what on earth is all this?'

Lucy was at home for the weekend, and she stood in the bathroom doorway, watching me dousing laundry in a bath full of Jeyes fluid.

'I know what you're going to say, Luce, but it must be done. It's mainly Gordon's stuff, and Aunt Helen's nighties, that sort of thing, but I'm disinfecting it all to be safe.'

Lucy sat on the toilet seat looking appalled.

'But it's awful that you should have to do this... surely the Council collects infected linen and autoclaves it or something? I mean... TB, Mum...'

'Yes, darling, I know.'

I pulled the plug in the bath and the grey soapy liquid drained thankfully away.

'But I'm really careful, I promise. Sheets and things do go off for decontamination; they provide big yellow plastic sacks for it, clearly marked, but as I say, most of this belongs to Gordon anyway.'

I ran the taps for the first rinse, wiping my brow with the bottom of my apron. This was my least favourite job.

'Why in heavens name do *you* have to do his washing, Mum? I mean, honestly, of all people! I bet he never even says thank you! What are *those*?'

She came over to peer at the old nylon pyjamas, circa 1960, that I squeezed out and lay in the bowl to be hung outside to dry.

Lately I had collected, washed, ironed and returned all personal and non-infected laundry from Elmwood, and much to my disgust, as Lucy had suspected, I never received as much as a simple thank you from Gordon. There was no contact at all from Aunt Helen, which worried me greatly, but it seemed that every effort we made to reach her was hastily thwarted by Gordon on some pretext or another. I even began to wonder whether he ever told Aunt Helen of our enquiries, or visits, while he kept her hidden away upstairs. I also supplied regular meals, such as the one-portion casseroles for Auntie Pearl, which I suspected were all consumed by Gordon alone. Aunt Helen, I was told on every visit, was confined to bed upstairs, unable to see any of us at any time.

The house was a sad disgrace. No one called any longer to clean, or tend the once-beautiful garden. A wonderful young chap called Sam came occasionally on his bike, to do odd maintenance jobs, and I remembered him, having been introduced to him about a year before by Aunt Helen. He was there one day when I called with clean laundry, his bike propped in the porch.

Sam opened the door to me when I rang the bell.

'Hi… Maggie, isn't it?' he smiled warmly. 'I'm here to clean the car and fix a couple of broken sashes on the windows. Are you coming in?'

I wrinkled my nose at the pungent smell of stale cat pee, and Sam grinned knowingly, but was far too polite to comment.

'Lady Helen's up in bed,' he said.

'Yes, I gather she doesn't get up any more, Sam. Have you seen her at all?'

He shook his head, his somewhat long, shiny hair flopping over his eyes.

'Not for months now, no. Gordon says no one can see her because of infection or something. I only work downstairs when I come.'

At that point Gordon appeared from the breakfast room, a tin of cat food in his hand and two strays at his heels, rubbing themselves around his grubby trouser legs. He bent to scoop the jellied meat out of the tin with a fork, refilling a rather grubby bowl which sat in the hallway beside a tray of foul-smelling cat litter.

'Ah, Maggie,' he said in acknowledgement. 'You can take that washing through to the dining room; there's another bag ready for you in there.'

I did so, wondering when Aunt Helen had last seen her lovely table, now littered with opened letters, old newspapers and goodness knows what. Two or three mugs containing cold dregs of tea or coffee stood on the dusty walnut wood, once shiny, and now stained with rings from the mugs amongst other things.

'Gordon, I would like to pop up and see Aunt Helen,' I said. 'I'm not afraid of infection. I just want to see her briefly. I've brought her these carnations…'

'No, no… can't be done.'

He was most emphatic, taking the flowers from me as he spoke. 'No visitors, no one at all. Helen's express wish. I'll give her these.'

'Well, I've written a note, just in case, actually.' I said, feeling annoyed. 'Perhaps you'd give that to her too.'

I dug around in my basket and brought out a cake tin containing fruit buns and a plastic box of stew.

'This is for you, Gordon, and there's a container here of soup for Aunt Helen. It's mushroom; I made it yesterday.'

'Take that in the kitchen then,' he said ungratefully, and I did, observing the state of the place with horror. I left my note, in a sealed envelope for Aunt Helen, on the table. In it I had expressed our love and real concern for her, and told her of the many enquiries we were all making on a regular basis for her; and how sad we were not to be able to see her, or speak to her on the phone, on Gordon's orders.

There were so many notes, cards and letters. As a family, we sent them to Aunt Helen regularly, expressing our love for her, and our wishes for her recovery, although we all really expected that this was not a possibility. It was so 'out of character' that we never received any reply to our letters or calls; we assumed that Aunt Helen felt too unwell to write, and that Gordon failed to pass on any messages she may have given him for us.

Brian spoke to her doctor on the phone, and met with a cautious response, causing him to wonder what impression of the family the fellow had been given. Had Gordon, perhaps, told him that we were an uncaring family, keen to be free of responsibility, which was far from the case? The doctor confirmed our fears that Helen was not expected to live very much longer, and that Gordon Lench had undertaken all care at home. Apparently he had qualified himself as next-of-kin, through whom all decisions were to be made. The doctor had considered taking out a court order to have Helen taken into nursing care in isolation, because he met with such resistance from Gordon, but discounted this as it wasn't Helen's wish to leave her home and her beloved cats.

There was little more we could do.

One evening in late November, Brian called at Elmwood and insisted most firmly on going upstairs to see Aunt Helen, albeit briefly. Gordon, true to form, was aggressive and angry, but Brian pushed past him and ran up the stairs two at a time.

Aunt Helen was sitting, propped up in bed by pillows, with two cats on her eiderdown asleep beside her. She saw Brian standing in the doorway, and her frail, pale little face... so thin, he said... broke into a smile.

'Brian! Where have you all been?' she asked pitifully. 'Why hasn't anyone come?'

Brian, shocked, told her at once that Gordon had kept us all away. That we were phoning often, and writing letters...

At which point, Gordon appeared behind him in the doorway, lighting his pipe and causing Aunt Helen to cough mercilessly.

'See what you've done!' shouted Gordon. 'I *told* you she wasn't well enough to see you! Now that's *enough*!'

Brian left, trembling with shock and rage, and deeply saddened. The months went by, the laundry continued, and to all intents and purposes, all contact with Aunt Helen herself was severed.

Many times the telephone rang and rang, unanswered, so we continued to write letters and sent flowers and little parcels... a tin of talcum powder (her favourite lavender); a soft flannel, a book of kittens... none of which were acknowledged.

Christmas came and went, without the usual cards, and understandably no gifts; though ours to Aunt Helen were all delivered to Elmwood by hand, and received disinterestedly, by Gordon.

Whenever we enquired, several times a week, Gordon told us she was worse.

'The man is mad,' I told Brian after one particularly distressing visit, when Gordon had literally barred the way at the foot of the stairs, and I had left feeling seriously afraid.

'You don't think... he couldn't... you don't think she's died, do you, and he hasn't said anything? You know, just left her lying there...'

Brian laughed awkwardly, but he wasn't amused.

'Good Lord no, Mags! Of course not. You and your imagination!'

Two nights later, the phone rang at 1 a.m. It was Gordon, his voice racked with sobs. Brian took the call, sitting on the side of our bed in the dark, while I struggled to find the switch on the bedside lamp.

'She's gone, I think she's gone,' Gordon was saying. 'I've called an ambulance, but I think she's finally gone…'

'OK, Gordon, we're coming over. We'll be with you very soon. It's OK, we're on our way now.'

It was the beginning of February, and the frost had already formed on the roads and car windows as we left home fifteen minutes later. As we drew up outside Elmwood we could see lights on in the house, and an ambulance parked by the tall wrought-iron gate, its rear doors open, but no one in sight.

The front door stood wide open, and much commotion was coming from upstairs.

We found Gordon slumped in the upstairs kitchen, whiskey bottle in hand, and tears rolling down his face, catching in the stubble on his unshaven cheeks.

In the bedroom, paramedics were attempting, ridiculously given her medical condition, to revive Aunt Helen on the floor. There were no cats to be seen, all of whom had scampered off for refuge under Gordon's bed or elsewhere.

'Don't! Please don't!' I begged, frustrated at the lack of dignity and respect for an eighty-nine year old lady with tuberculosis, whom we loved.

'Got to try, love, when we're called out,' one paramedic in green overalls explained. 'It's the law; got to have a go.'

'But she's eighty-nine, and she has TB! Please, just let her be,' I asked, and they finally stopped their futile banging, thumping and blowing.

'Thank you. I understand why you had to try. But it's really not on,' I explained.

Aunt Helen's body was taken to St Mary's Hospital in Roehampton, and we followed the ambulance in our car, with Gordon in the back, aggressive with the mixture of grief and alcohol. I attempted to comfort him by putting my arm around his shoulders when he was sitting on a small hospital chair in an ante-room allocated to us by a kindly nurse, but he shoved me away with such a thump that my ribs were bruised.

It interested and astonished us that Gordon claimed vehemently to be the next-of-kin, and signed the necessary forms, although Brian mentioned to the nurse that he was a nephew and executor.

We waited while a pleasant, kindly girl washed Aunt Helen's frail little body and laid her out in a white paper hospital shroud, and then we were allowed to see her and say our last goodbyes. She looked at peace, and I smoothed her thin grey hair, not recently washed or brushed. Sadly, I wished so much that we had been involved in caring for her properly at the end, instead of being forbidden any access.

We then drove Gordon home to Elmwood and promised to contact him the next day. I suspected that he spent the rest of the night in the company of the remainder of the whisky bottle, in the filthy little upstairs kitchen.

Brian wanted to arrange the funeral, given that choices had already been made and recorded, and all that was required was to organise and put Aunt Helen's wishes into place. He spent many hours dealing with these arrangements, and collecting the necessary forms to fulfil his duties as planned.

It was while he was dealing with this, in his role as executor and nephew, that the first blow concerning the will was dealt. Brian had been to Elmwood to discuss details with Gordon one afternoon in the week following Helen's death, and he returned home looking angry and shaken. I heard the car pull up in front of our house and the driver's door bang as he got out; I was in our sitting room watching the television news, and I looked up as the front door opened.

'Hey, what's wrong? Darling, you look awful…'

I went to him at once, for our usual welcome kiss, and gave him a hug instead.

'I'm so cross, Mags… you won't believe this!' He threw down his leather driving gloves onto the sideboard in the hall with a smack.

'That wretched man has been meddling as I feared, you know; can you ever imagine what he told me tonight?'

'What, for heaven's sake?'

'Apparently I am *not* any longer Aunt Helen's executor... no, that's right... Gordon told me it was a changed in September, no less; and guess who has taken over in my place?'

'No! Not Gordon! Brian, he can't have!'

He was nodding furiously.

'Yes, indeed, I'm afraid so. I'm really furious, Mags, and it won't have been Aunt Helen's wish to change it, I'm sure of that. How dare he... and you know what? He's changed the will! I took my copy of the one we did together, Aunt Helen and I, with Will Rogers, the solicitor in Sheen.'

'I remember she liked him; she said she didn't trust that other local fellow in Barnes...'

'Exactly! Wallace Beasby. Who, incidentally, is an old buddy of Gordon's. Well, would you credit it, a new will was drawn up in September... why wasn't it ever mentioned to me?... using Wallace Beasby instead of Will Rogers. And Gordon is named as co-executor with the solicitor. A solicitor, bear in mind, whom Aunt Helen did *not* like! Now, is that all a bit odd, or what?'

I sat heavily down on the sofa, not sure of what to do with myself, so angry and confused as I felt.

'Oh Brian... it's all wrong... I'm sure it is. What about all those hours and evenings you spent running through everything with Aunt Helen, and she never seemed troubled then, did she?'

He shook his head wearily.

'Never at all; not one bit. Everything she wanted, all her plans and arrangements... it's all been changed. I just don't think she even knew; maybe too ill to understand...' My memory was working overtime, and I picked up on something Brian had mentioned a few minutes ago.

'Bri... didn't you tell me just now that it was altered in September? That's about four months or so ago; the time that Gordon started to block all our contact with Aunt Helen! Perhaps that was partly why... so she never found out, or if she did know, she would have told you. Considering the number of times she used to ask you over just to run through everything, don't you think it strange that she never mentioned any changes to you?'

Brian nodded, his face ashen.

'Thing is, Mags,' he said quietly, 'we can't prove it. Can't prove a thing. Perhaps the least said the better, d'you think?'

I was glad that the children were not at home, as it would not have been good for them to have witnessed their normally calm, stable father so angry and upset.

And there was more to come, we discovered subsequently... much more.

The funeral should have been a special occasion. Aunt Helen had talked to Brian several times about the sort of service she would like when the time came, and he made every effort to fulfil her wishes as he tried to make the necessary arrangements. This was of course, extremely difficult as he and Gordon were not on good terms since the disclosure about changes in the will and the executorship. We knew Aunt Helen had wanted a service akin to Uncle Tom's, in the same church in Barnes, and there were many people living locally who would have come. There were folk involved with the Wildlife group Aunt Helen had founded, neighbours who loved her and old friends, to say nothing of us, the family.

However, it was not to be. Control had been removed from Brian, and Gordon took over all decisions regardless of the wishes of the family, and indeed, as we were sure, of Aunt Helen herself. He organised just a simple cremation at Mortlake, on a miserable, cold February afternoon. Gordon read the eulogy, and walked behind the coffin... one he had chosen, covered in flowers he had ordered from himself. Our family wreaths lay separately. He looked a broken man, that day, and I noticed he had cut himself shaving... there was a small nick under one ear, and a slither of dried blood rested on his neck. Some of us returned to Elmwood afterwards for tea.

Louise and I made cakes and sandwiches, and a kind neighbour called Molly from along the lane was at the house with kettles boiling for tea when we arrived. I spoke to her in the kitchen. 'Molly, you're a star. Thank you so much for this.'

She shrugged, giving me a cautious glance over her purple-framed glasses. 'It's the least I could do,' she said quietly. 'I was very fond of Lady Helen. And Sir Tom, you know… very fond. Such a gentleman, he was, and very good to our Tony. They'd have been the same age, he and their Malcolm. Terrible sadness, that. The boys used to play together, down by the river when they were young. Fishing, and what have you, you know. I was fond of them here, then.'

'Well, it's really nice of you to help us here today. I'm sorry though, if it meant you couldn't be at the cremation.'

We were pouring tea in the breakfast room from two large pots, and Louise was taking the delicate china cups around on a tray in the drawing room.

'No more!' she said, returning some untouched. 'Less people than we'd expected, Mags. We don't need all these. Here, have one yourself. And you, Molly.'

'I was just saying,' Molly continued, now clearly in full flow. 'I'm glad to help today for Lady Helen, you understand.' She lowered her voice checking furtively for anyone in earshot by the door.

'But not for him… oh dear me, no, certainly not for him.'

She inclined her head towards the hallway, where we could hear Gordon's low tones in conversation with Ted and Maud.

'In fact,' Molly continued, 'this will be the last time I come here, this will. I'll be leaving my key when I go. I've always kept one, since Lady Helen gave it to me when she lived alone, just in case, you know. But I'll not be coming here again, that's for sure.'

She rubbed her hands on her apron as though it was a *fait accompli*, and sat down heavily on one of the cats' chairs.

Louise and I perched cautiously on the edge of the long kitchen sideboard, keen to hear more. She winked at me knowingly.

'Gordon, you mean, Molly; he's the problem, I take it?'

Molly nodded fervently, her grey curls… an old perm which had grown out… waggling around her face.

'Everyone around here would say so; I'm not alone. Not many neighbours here today, are there? We'd all have come, but for him. He kept us all away you know, and then said it was 'family only' at the funeral.'

I was aghast.

'Molly! He didn't? That wasn't anyone's wish!'

'Well, it certainly was his, I can tell you. Muriel Briggs at number eleven called to offer her condolences last week and was sent away sharpish without so much as a thank you.'

I nibbled at a sandwich.

'Has Gordon always been unpopular in the lane?' I asked.

'You've known him for years, Molly, haven't you?'

'Well, I should say so. His wife Florrie was a lovely soul, bless her, I got on well with her. Their boy Paul was the same age as Tony too, and even in those days, Gordon was a pig of a man, you know. He didn't treat that lad well, not well at all.'

Empty cups were gradually being returned to the kitchen, and Louise went into the hall to say goodbyes as people left. I filled the sink with soapy water, and Molly and I began to wash up.

'I don't understand, Molly,' I said, wrist-deep in bubbles. She stood with a tea towel on which were printed cats of all colours, and dried the dainty silver teaspoons one by one.

'How did Aunt Helen become so fond of a friend no one else ever liked? We all loved her, you know, and things seemed to change so much after Uncle Tom died.'

Suddenly Molly's expression changed, and she went quiet.

'Not my place to say,' she muttered. 'Just be sure I'll never come here ever again, Maggie. He's dangerous, that man, mark my words.'

As we left the house, the sharp, cold wind blew under our thick winter coats, and the little wooden cross marked 'Susie' was clearly visible under the trees. I commented to my mother-in-law that we hadn't seen any cats in the house. She took me by the arm and propelled me through the tall wrought-iron gate, without even a glance behind her. Gordon was framed in the doorway, formally shaking my father-in-law's hand, looking every bit the master of the house.

Maud was obviously upset.

'Never mind the cats,' she said. 'I dare say they're all shut up upstairs for safety. Some of them never go out; that's why those dreadful litter trays are everywhere, I suppose.'

We unlocked the car and sat together in the back, leaving the front for Brian and Ted.

'Well, that's that then,' Maud said in true matter-of-fact Yorkshire fashion. 'End of an era. I doubt we'll ever go to Elmwood again now, especially if that Gordon's here.'

Said with feeling.

Louise and David were helping Auntie Pearl into their car, and I noticed sadly how crippled she was, and how much worse the arthritis had become in recent months. They all waved as they drove off.

Our children, all present at the crematorium, had left after the service and not returned to the house, along with Louise and David's two sons, Peter and Stuart.

How few of us, it seemed, had come here to remember a dear aunt, a loved sister-in-law, a valued friend and neighbour. What a comparison with Uncle Tom's funeral, and what a shame and a sadness.

Brian and his father came out to the car carrying cake tins of mine and some unfinished sandwiches.

'Darling, you could have left those for Gordon,' I said, taking them onto my lap in the back seat.

'I did,' he said. 'Plenty there still. Just so few of us to eat them... I said you'd done too many.'

We drove away from Elmwood quietly. End of an era, as Maud had said. I couldn't help reflecting on how different it should have been.

Chapter Six

'My God, I'm so angry, Mags. I just feel so abused, somehow. I can't get my head around this... I mean, how dare the man do this, of all things...'

Brian spluttered with rage as we drove along the M25 on our return from supper with my cousins one Saturday evening. His knuckles were white as he gripped the steering wheel. It was always the case; whenever we discussed what had happened with others, who were naturally inquisitive and interested, it left us facing the situation head on in our minds once more, and Brian, especially, was outraged.

The week after the funeral had been a telling time. Gordon remained in the house, lying low, seemingly out of contact with us. He didn't answer the phone, made no attempt to be in touch with us, nor indeed, anyone else, to our knowledge. Brian decided to visit, to establish what was to be done about Aunt Helen's will.

March had arrived with a flourish, the frost and slight peppering of snow in February completely gone. Wintry sunshine crept through the brown branches of the trees surrounding Elmwood, and the cold winds gave way to a spring-like warmth in the air. There were tiny snowdrops in the garden, a sure sign of spring on the way.

Brian and I, still mystified about the recent events surrounding Aunt Helen's death, called by arrangement with Gordon one Saturday afternoon. Rowing crews flashed by the bottom of Elmwood's garden, practising keenly on the river for the new season's events to come, in particular the Head of the River race scheduled for the following weekend.

In contrast, Elmwood itself was far from busy. Cats lay sleeping peacefully, curled up here and there in luxurious abandon, unaware of the state of increasing squalor which surrounded them indoors. The stench was overpowering; I suspected that windows and doors were never opened, and fresh air never circulated to clear the fog of tobacco smoke and stale cat pee.

Gordon's ladder still stood against the garden wall, but now at a rakish angle, suggesting that it had been unused for some time.

Brian had a house key, and we let ourselves in when there was no response to our ringing of the doorbell. We wondered whether Gordon had forgotten our arrangement.

We found him, eventually, asleep in the upstairs kitchen, slumped over the table, a cold cup of tea and the remains of a paltry lunch on the table beside him.

'Gordon? Gordon, it's us… Brian and Maggie. Are you all right?'

Despite his anger about the will, Brian showed his usual care and concern on finding this sad old man in such a state. We noticed that his clothes were dirty and dishevelled, he was unshaven again, and he looked generally unkempt.

'Eh? Oh, is that you, then? Must have dropped off… how did you get in?'

Gordon stood, shakily, to greet us, and I sensed that his lunch had been washed down by a considerable amount of whisky.

'We used my key,' Brian said. 'And the bolt wasn't set inside… had you been out this morning, and not secured it when you came in?'

Gordon shook his head and adjusted his hearing aid. He often missed a lot of what was said – sometimes, I felt, deliberately. Brian decided not to pursue the point, and I was staying quiet, aware that Gordon had neither time nor patience for me, a mere woman. He had become increasingly chauvinistic and was often downright rude. Needless to say, I was no longer doing his laundry, nor providing him with home-cooked meals and baking, all of which had previously been unappreciated.

Brian pulled up two chairs to the table for us to sit down, removing heaps of papers and on one, old rags of dubious use.

'Gordon, we've come over so that I can talk to you about Aunt Helen's will,' he explained. 'Amongst other things, of course. Like what you plan to do now, and the arrangements for the house, and so on.'

'Shall I make some tea?' I suggested bravely, since the crockery around us looked decidedly suspicious.

'No milk, I ran out this morning.' Gordon said, hardly bothered. 'Depends if you like your tea black or not. I'm not worried either way, myself.'

We decided not to risk it, and I left the two men to their discussion and went for a wander around the house to assess the 'state of play.'

To my horror, Aunt Helen's bedroom appeared to have been virtually untouched since the night of her death. The bedlinen was dirty and dishevelled, the commode unemptied. There was a rank smell hanging in the air; the once-lovely deep velvet curtains drawn as if to keep out the sun or the freshness of the outside world. Here and there a cat lurked, using the filthy carpet as a litter tray in several places. Coco, Gordon's own perky little black cat, lay curled in a cosy ball on the sofa beneath the window, oblivious to the horrors surrounding her. A blood-stained pink woollen bedjacket lay abandoned in a heap in an armchair, upon which lay another black cat, older and mangy, with patches of missing fur and one torn ear – from fighting, I supposed.

Even Aunt Helen's last meagre meal tray lay abandoned and untouched on the bedside table; a piece of what may have been bread and marmalade crawling with flies.

I went at once back to the small kitchen and confronted Gordon gently.

'We really must do something about the bedroom,' I said, sitting on the chair previously stacked with newspapers. 'How can I help you, Gordon? It's dreadful in there, and it's got to be done.'

He looked such a sad, broken old man, obviously struggling alone with his grief. He must have been somewhat more than a friend to Aunt Helen I felt, looking anxiously at Brian. I knew he felt the same. Always a gentle, compassionate man, his anger with Gordon was on a back burner, so to speak, while we were with him, watching his deep distress, and his inability to cope.

'Maybe we could tackle it for you now,' Brian suggested. 'Let's bundle everything for disposal into those yellow sacks marked 'danger', to be on the safe side, and then it can be arranged that they're collected by the Council.'

'I'm surprised that the district nurse hasn't been about all of that,' I commented. 'There are all Aunt Helen's medicines to be disposed of correctly as well; they usually come round to help deal with that sort of thing after a death.'

Gordon huffed, annoyed.

'Well, some stupid woman did call, a few days ago, and I sent her packing at once, I can tell you. She tried to come inside and I gave her a sharp slap on the doorstep. She soon beat a retreat!'

Typical, I thought. We set to work, leaving Gordon to his whisky and his misery.

'What about all the official things?' I asked Brian in a low voice, behind the bedroom door. 'What'll happen about the will?'

'I'll tell you in the car.' Brian's voice was subdued and serious, but neither of us wanted to chat while we worked amongst such degradation and awfulness. We cleared the room as quickly as we could on the surface, and subsequently arranged for a special council disposal van to collect all bedding, the mattress and anything soiled, as it was contaminated and dangerous material. I washed over all the surfaces with disinfectant, and vacuumed the horrendously stained carpet.

'These drawers are all full of Aunt Helen's personal things,' I commented, opening the top one in a beautiful George I tallboy chest.

Gordon appeared, unstable, in the doorway, whisky bottle in one hand.

'Yes,' he growled at me, 'and you will leave everything untouched, Maggie! Close that drawer at once! I'll not have you meddling in her things, do you understand?'

Taken aback, I pushed the drawer closed and declined to respond. Soon afterwards we left, and I understood Molly the neighbour's feelings of never wishing to return, while Gordon was at the house.

'So, tell me about the will,' I urged Brian as we drove out of Gumber Lane. His left eyebrow twitched, a sure sign of his annoyance.

'The man is a fiend,' he said. 'I can't get over it, I really can't. I'm going to take legal advice on this one, Mags; it's all completely alien to Aunt Helen's wishes. Clearly what Gordon's done is to withdraw the services of Will Rogers in Sheen and employ that rogue Wallace Beasby who's his old mate... they've drawn up a new will and somehow got poor old Helen to sign just before she died. It gives Gordon the right to live on at Elmwood until his death, all bills to be paid from her estate, mind you, and it's in order if you please, to care for the cats! There's a fairly substantial sum mentioned for Gordon, otherwise no one inherits a single thing, Mags... can you believe that?'

'Never! Oh, Bri, what about Auntie Pearl? She needs her regular support money... Aunt Helen always gave her that! And what about your Mum and Dad? All those Fawley things at the house... they should rightfully belong to your father now. Who gets those?'

He sighed deeply.

'Absolutely everything goes to the Cats' Charity, along with the house. Not a single tin whistle for any of us, not a single thing, Mags. It's just unbelievable.'

He swerved to avoid a motorcyclist, and I saw that he was shaking.

'Well, what about all the furniture? You know, the things Louise and I had to choose, and Aunt Helen made those lists with us. Surely that still stands... she can't have changed her mind like this, right at the end!'

'Well, I'm sure she didn't. I'm going to try to see a copy of this new will and compare it with the original one I've got at home. There's something very wrong been going on, of that I'm certain. I'll get to the bottom of it, Mags, you see if I don't.'

The whole family was affected by the amazing changes to Aunt Helen's will. Never people to be grasping for money, or to 'demand their rights', so to speak, the Fawleys were quietly shocked and saddened that our memories in the future of Aunt Helen should be marred by the outcome of what must have been Gordon's actions. In private we were all angry; publicly, we all wore acceptance with good grace. We fell short of finding a reason why, a purpose that Gordon could have had, in making such manipulative and dramatic changes to the wishes of a lady who trusted him completely as a dear friend of long standing.

Gradually, our contact with Elmwood lessened and it was only Brian who called occasionally over the next months, wanting as he did, to ascertain the course of things concerning our former family house and belongings. Aunt Helen had died without any living relatives other than the Fawley family; no one on her own side remained. It seemed, too, that any old friends she may have had, had faded away over the years since Uncle Tom's death.

'Probably put off by Gordon,' I suggested one evening, as we sat with glasses of wine in a Maidenhead pub on the river. The summer was warm, and the evening air thick with tiny thunder flies. We watched a family of ducks gently meandering past the pub's low wall, the river in their wake gently lapping at the bank.

'Very sad, whatever the reason,' Brian commented. 'I think the two of them were always very sociable when Uncle Tom was alive, in the early days.' He flicked a midge out of his wine and wiped his fingers on the edge of the wooden patio table.

'But then, as I remember, after Malcolm's death things changed, and we certainly didn't see either of them much at home after that. I was only young though... maybe I've forgotten.'

'You would remember, Bri, if there had been regular occasions when they'd joined your parents. And Auntie Pearl too, they'd been so close to her. I think it's very odd.'

'I remember Uncle Tom and Dad going off on boating holidays together. Just a week each time; I think they enjoyed fishing. But Mum and Aunt Helen and we kids never went with them.'

'I wonder if Gordon's friendship with Aunt Helen was going strong then,' I mused. 'And whether he was as friendly with Uncle Tom as he was with her?'

Brian shrugged.

'Never really thought about it,' he said.

'Hmm. I bet your mother did.' I smiled, knowing that she would never have talked about it, whatever she thought. My mother-in-law was about as closed as a closed book could be when it came to what she would call gossip, and we all respected her for that.

'Should we tell your parents, do you think, about our meeting next week? Would it upset them?'

'Best left unmentioned, I would say,' Brian nodded. 'They might be fine about it, but until we know the outcome... yes, best not to say.'

Louise and David, Brian and I, had an appointment with a Mr Vic Towers, of the Cats' Charity, to discuss the bequest and voice our concern and distress. Not least the manner in which alterations had been made so close to Aunt Helen's death, which we knew were in no way her own wishes.

Vic Towers greeted us at the door of the charity's head office; a greying, welcoming man in a green mottled jumper and a pair of corduroy trousers, well clawed around the knees.

We sat around a low coffee table on old chintz armchairs, in a sunny office on the outskirts of Brighton. The journey there had been blisteringly hot and our car lacked air-conditioning. Louise looked less than comfortable when we arrived, and was glad of the pot of coffee and jug of orange squash on the table for our refreshment.

David and Brian gave Vic Towers the general picture of the situation, having previously sent him details by post, and he already seemed familiar with the story.

'I'm truly sorry,' he said, 'It's a shocking scenario for the family. I understand there are genuine needs on the parts of Lady Helen's brother-in-law and sisters-in-law, and it does seem more than surprising that these should have been overlooked, given that provision had been made for them in the previous will.'

'I was always Aunt Helen's executor,' Brian explained. 'And I was with her at the solicitor's of her choice when she drew up her original will. Totally different, I might say, from the present one. None of us can understand what happened between the time last winter when she was diagnosed with virulent TB, and her death in early February. That was the time that Gordon kept her bedridden in her room and determinedly excluded anyone from the house. That, incidentally, was when the will was changed… manipulated, we feel by Gordon himself, and unknown to any of us until after Aunt Helen's death.'

Vic Towers shook his head as if in disbelief, but then went on to say:

'Not unusual, I'm sad to say. I see such things as this all the time, here. I believe we are one of the richest charities, if not the richest charity in Great Britain, with so many old ladies especially, leaving us their all. And there's always an aggrieved relative, believe me, often with good cause. I have a copy of Lady Fawley's will here…'

As beneficiary, the charity had received word some months before of the legacy and its interesting stipulations. Vic rustled about in a blue box file and extracted his copy of Aunt Helen's will. We had also perused it, as Louise and David's younger son Stuart (a solicitor) had obtained a copy for us from the Probate Office.

Vic scratched his chin as he read it, through horn-rimmed spectacles taken from his shirt pocket.

'Hmm… not an easy one, this,' he said thoughtfully. 'Not at all straightforward. You may be aware that we've hit a problem already with the neighbours in Gumber Lane…'

Louise smirked, pouring us all some orange squash.

'Oh yes, we know all about that,' she said. 'The petition, you mean?'

'Yes, that's right. I believe it was all reported in the press. The snag is that delighted as we are to be given such a lovely house, the will stipulates that the garden must be used as a cat sanctuary, so we can't just sell the property and bank a hefty cheque.'

We were all aware of the situation, and had indeed seen the newspapers and even local television coverage.

'Well, the neighbours' petition has put paid to that, we understand,' said Brian. 'Not the sort of thing anyone in a leafy lane in Barnes would welcome really. So where does that leave the charity, Vic?'

Vic shrugged his shoulders and removed his spectacles, replacing them carefully in his breast pocket. He folded his copy of the will and put it back in the blue box file before he replied. One gained the impression that he did nothing quickly.

'Where indeed!' he sighed. 'One day in the future, no doubt, we shall be considerably better off, but for the time being we await the result of the planning permission for a cattery, and given local opposition to such a scheme, that's most unlikely to be granted.' He leant back in his chair and slowly crossed his legs.

'In that event,' he went on, 'we shall be forced to wait until Gordon Lench's death, and then place the property on the market. In many years' time, possibly.'

David, sitting patiently for the right moment to speak, now coughed to herald his comments. He sat forward in his chair, leaning his elbows on his knees.

'Vic, I think we ought to talk about the family here,' he said. 'Something seriously overlooked, we feel. Especially as Aunt Helen's wishes... her original wishes, are most certainly not being honoured. Where would we stand if we were to stake a claim of some sort, do you think?'

Vic smiled kindly.

'Sadly, I think you can do extremely little,' he said. 'If you were a dependant next of kin and could prove such, you might have a case, and the charity would want to look favourably at it. But as you stand, I'm afraid you're left in the cold, so to speak.'

Brian was prepared for this.

'Vic, there's a small matter of furniture here,' he explained. 'The house is full of really valuable antiques, which had previously been allocated by my aunt to the four of us here. Lists were made some years ago, with Aunt Helen, and I know she was anxious that certain items remained in the family. There are two longcase clocks which she specially wanted us to have, and she made notes to that effect and placed them inside each clock some time ago. Recently I showed these to Gordon at the house and he was clearly shaken. I don't think he had discussed this with Aunt Helen at all. He told me that any of her wishes on paper—'

'And it's obviously her own handwriting... ' I butted in.

Brian gave me a serious 'look' for disturbing his train of thought, and continued:

'Any of her written notes are now irrelevant as the new will states otherwise. Can't anything be done about that, do you suppose?'

Vic looked uncomfortable. I felt sorry for him, faced with the four of us, all feeling angry with the situation, but it was not his fault we were angry and unhappy.

'Well, no... legally I don't believe it can,' he said, in response to Brian's question.

'What I've done before, however, in this sort of instance, is to make a special gift on behalf of the charity to a family member; where an item is a personal treasure, for example; perhaps we could do that here.'

And so it was that arrangements were agreed for our two clocks to be offered to the family at the appropriate time in the future, when Elmwood and all its contents became available for sale. And that time, it was to become clear, was only when Gordon Lench released his new-found hold on the house, and all of our family belongings within. It was a bitter pill to swallow.

Chapter Seven

The grand days of Elmwood were over. In the months and indeed, years that followed Aunt Helen's death, our contact with Gordon dwindled to almost nothing. Christmas cards were exchanged and there was the very occasional telephone call such as the time when the house was burgled.

I was sewing rabbit buttons on a tiny white cardigan, knitted amidst much excitement as we awaited the birth of our first grandchild, who proved to be a beautiful daughter for James and Lesley. Brian answered the phone in the hall and returned to me in the sunshine on the patio. It was late July, 1999.

'Well, what do you think of that!' he exclaimed. 'It was old Gordon on the phone… he's had burglars at Elmwood.'

I put down my needle and looked up, over the rim of my new glasses.

'Oh no, Bri! What's been taken?' I said, immediately thinking of all the family treasures that, if things had been different, would have been safely stored in our home and Louise's now.

'Quite a bit of the silver, he thinks; trinkets and small items really. All the lovely stuff on that card table in the French windows. I always said it was asking for trouble to leave that laid out so obviously there for all to see.'

I huffed.

'Who is 'all', Bri? No one ever passes that window… it's at the back. Actually, no one passing the house would see inside anyway; there's a long drive and all those trees to hide the windows at the front. And who ever goes round to the back through the garden?'

'You never know. Anyway, I doubt if Gordon would be aware. I think he virtually lives upstairs these days, in his bedroom, and that top kitchen. The downstairs rooms are all closed up.'

Brian started to pull up weeds in our rose beds beside the patio while I sewed.

'There! How's that for a little tiddler?' I held up my handiwork, taking pleasure in Brian's smile of delighted anticipation. 'Roll on, baby. We're all ready for you.'

'I'd better go over to Elmwood, I suppose,' Brian pondered. 'Just to take a look, and see if Gordon's OK. He sounded pretty shaken.'

'It will have been upsetting to find things missing,' I agreed. 'I take it Gordon was at home at the time?'

Brian nodded.

'Apparently so, but he can't tell when it happened. Like I said, the rooms were closed up downstairs, and it seems the thieves gained entry via the French windows and only took things from the drawing room. They didn't seem to have come through to the hall at all, so it was only by chance that Gordon discovered the theft when he was in the garden yesterday, checking the cat shelters, and he spotted the broken window.'

'All those lovely things, Bri, what a crying shame. And Fawley things at that. I really wish nothing had been left like it has; just as if time had stopped, you know. Those rooms must be rank and dusty, unused and all locked up. And all your family treasures taken now… did Gordon call the police?'

'Oh yes,' Brian grinned. 'I gather a couple of police women came… big mistake! He told me he gave them a piece of his mind and as you would expect he maligned them dreadfully and sent them packing. In his words they were worse than useless without half a brain between them!'

'Glad I wasn't there. He is so rude, that man, especially to women. No wonder he's so lonely.'

I went inside to prepare our supper and Brian followed, washing soil from his hands in the kitchen sink.

We had long since abandoned the idea of taking any responsibility for Gordon; we were in no way related and had never developed even a friendly relationship with him. All contact in Aunt Helen's days had been for her sake and we saw less and less of the old man after the upset over the will. The Cats' Charity seemed to have taken a back seat, having assumed ownership of Elmwood following the legacy, and they were simply waiting for Gordon's death one day in the future, to take responsibility for dealing with the property and its contents. They were informed of the burglary, but apparently seemed unconcerned. No doubt Vic Towers and his colleagues felt such a thing was almost inevitable, and having taken an initial inventory for probate, they weren't showing interest until such time as the house was free for them to take over.

Brian went to see Gordon at Elmwood the next evening. I stayed at home, waiting in case of a phone call to say Lesley was in labour. He returned distressed by what he found, and we drank coffee with the ten o'clock television news.

'Mags, you wouldn't believe the house,' he said. 'I was shattered, honestly, to see it. The ceiling in the drawing room is looking terrible, with a huge patch of damp and the wallpaper all peeling off behind the piano. Gordon says it's the same in his bedroom above, so I should think there's a problem with that part of the roof; I promised to help him get someone in.'

'Heaven help whoever that is,' I muttered. 'What about the missing silver and things?'

'All gone,' he sighed. 'Thieves must have just come in and emptied everything transportable into a couple of large bags, and left again by the same French window. I boarded it up for Gordon while I was there, with old wood from the shed left from the cat shelters, but it's a bit of a shoddy job. He can't cope at all now, you know... I promised to get another guy in to fix the glass as well.'

'You are a good man, Brian Fawley,' I said, cuddling up under his arm on the sofa. 'Who else in all the world would be so gracious to a rude old pig who's treated you and all your family so appallingly?'

'Well, I just feel he's a pitiful old fool really,' Brian said. 'He seems to have no one in all the world. Any old friends he might have had when he was younger have either died, like Wallace Beasby last month, or disappeared over the years.'

'Well, I'm not at all surprised, knowing the way he treats people. Just look at what he said about the two policewomen who came...'

Brian laughed.

'There's a sequel to that,' he said. 'Someone... another girl... came today from Victim Support, I gather because he had reported a burglary and lives alone, and she too, was sent away in a cloud of verbal abuse, by all accounts. He really is an old rogue.'

'Rogue is not the word I'd use,' I mumbled. 'You know, I cannot imagine why he and Aunt Helen were such friends. She was so gentle and polite, and—'

'And he is just an old buffer, yes, I know. But he was never rude or difficult with her, was he?'

'Apart from constantly smoking his pipe, I suppose not; not that we ever witnessed, anyway. But have you ever met anyone else who's had a good word to say about him?'

Brian shrugged.

'I rest my case,' I said, with a smile.

The news came through the following week that our first little granddaughter had been born; an amazing, totally beautiful little bundle of joy and wonder with dark hair and big blue eyes just like her daddy. James was besotted in an instant, and they named her Emily. For a while our world was filled with nothing else but baby pleasure, and the only sadness for us was that my dear parents, and Brian's mother Maud who had died the previous year, were not alive to be great-grandparents. Ted, however, was delighted with his new role, especially as Emily arrived in time to be his ninetieth birthday present. He held her, sleeping peacefully, in his arms, stroking her soft, dark baby curls with his big, gentle hand. We took photos to be treasured always... a new little Fawley had arrived.

The windows at Elmwood were repaired, and the roof where the rain had poured in, damaging two ceilings and beautiful flocked paper walls. Nothing was done, however, to rectify the mess, and the ruined wallpaper was left to hang in dried and faded curls, looking for all the world as though no one cared. It was Gordon's decision to leave everything as it was... he would allow no one in to deal with the result of the damage other than the roof repairer and the glazier.

Number one Gumber Lane, Gordon's own house next door, was eventually sold, and a new young family with two top-of-the-range cars moved in. Before they arrived, however, Sam was summoned to transfer Gordon's belongings and some of his furniture, to Elmwood next door. Brian, always generous-hearted, felt he should help, and turned up with me on a Saturday morning in late autumn.

The leaves on the trees in the lane and the long gardens were falling fast, carpeting the ground in orange and brown. It was a windy day.

I zipped my fleece high around my neck and set to work in 'number one' to pack belongings into boxes for transferral. The state of the house was even worse than Elmwood had become, because Gordon, of course, had not lived here now for some years. Brian and I were annoyed to discover that in order to make room for some of his personal furniture, Gordon had auctioned several beautiful antiques belonging to Tom and Helen.

'It's an outrage!' I said quietly, as we staggered through the garden with a 1960s stereo set, totally out of place amongst the original grandeur of the Elmwood drawing room.

'Where is that gorgeous inlaid cabinet that was against the wall? Brian, there are several things missing... what has he done with the money?'

Brian shrugged.

'It's not our money, Mags,' he said. 'Nothing we can do about it. It's probably in his own account now, despite the fact that he certainly doesn't need it, knowing as I do what he got for his house. Too late now; forget it.'

That 'moving day' was horrendous, and we left Elmwood in the early evening feeling weary and dejected. We had piled hundreds, possibly thousands of old letters, newspapers and documents on the once-lovely walnut dining table, transferred from Gordon's cheap version in his dining room next door. These were stacked higgledy-piggledy over the surface of the table, giving it an air of the final minutes of a jumble sale. Everything we had moved in was a poor substitute for Aunt Helen's furniture, and the mixture of the two looked dreadful. The rooms however, were looking dreadful anyway; uncleaned and uncared for and for so long now. Gordon had no help in the house, mainly because he refused to tolerate women, and also because the state of things had gone beyond rectification.

The one room we didn't touch was the downstairs study, which had been Uncle Tom's; always locked in the past, and still locked and sealed now.

'Don't go in there!' Gordon had shouted, when I attempted to turn the key, thinking that it might be a better room to store all his papers. 'Don't ever go in there! Just leave all those in the dining room… I'll get around to dealing with them all eventually.'

I doubt it, I thought to myself, and indeed, he never did. Within weeks Gordon was on the telephone to Brian again, asking him to come over and help him with his paperwork; it all needed to be sorted and dealt with, he said, and it had got on top of him recently. Louise and I felt it would have been perfectly appropriate for Brian to refuse due to the pressure of work, but as always, in his kindness, he agreed to go.

On the evening of his visit, Gordon announced that he had appointed Brian as his executor, because he had no one else to ask, and Brian, feeling sorry for him, agreed. It was a minor, very minor, bone of contention between us, because I felt it was asking too much, and given all that had happened before, it was an imposition.

'Who else can he ask, then, Mags?' Brian argued his case. 'There doesn't seem to be a living soul, except me. Little enough to do for an old boy, I should have thought.'

'Little enough!' I was angry, and it was out of character for me to be angry, especially with Brian, whom I adored.

'Look at all you've done for Gordon already! And he never appreciates any of it at all. He's got worse, Bri, he's so grumpy and aggressive. He treats me disgracefully, you know he does.'

'Yes, I know, but that's because you're female… you shouldn't take it personally. God knows he's a poor old sod, and he really needs help sorting out all those old papers. There are loads of unpaid bills and so on amongst them; he really can't cope.'

The financier in my husband always came to the fore in these sort of situations and he was a true Fawley, just like his father, always keen to be of help.

'It won't take me that long, Mags, I promise,' he said.

How wrong he was.

Chapter Eight

The house next door at 'number one' was comprehensively renovated and tastefully modernised while retaining its original style, and the young family moved in.

Brian met Belinda Morris and her children as he was leaving Elmwood after one of his paperwork visits, and she was bundling the kids out of her people carrier having picked them up from Brownies. Two little girls, both in their brown and yellow uniforms ran inside squealing merrily, and Belinda hung back to introduce herself to Brian with a smile. She wore clean, tidy, denim jeans and a sharp red tee-shirt under her padded gilet, and she pushed her blonde hair behind one ear as she spoke.

'Hallo!' (offering an outstretched hand). 'I'm Belinda Morris, your new neighbour.'

Brian laughed.

'Good Lord, no, actually, I'm just a visitor,' he said, horrified that she had thought it possible that he lived in such a dilapidated house. He explained, and was met with an interested smile.

'Oh... I do remember quite a to-do a few years back, now you mention it,' she said. 'We lived on the outskirts of Hammersmith before, and it was all in the papers, wasn't it, about your aunt's will, and everything?'

'I'm afraid so. You'll only see me here occasionally now, when I come over to help Gordon with his bills and things. You have met him, haven't you?'

Belinda grimaced a little.

'Oh yes, most certainly we have. I'm afraid he doesn't like the children much... very grumpy about having children next door. No,' she corrected herself, 'not even next door, actually more in the road, he said! It's not as if we're very close, anyway, is it? Big detached houses like these two; they really are a good distance away from each other. Anyway, he wasn't at all pleased to meet us!'

Brian laughed.

'That'll be right. Typical Gordon… doesn't like women or children, especially female children! I'm sorry.'

Was it any wonder that Gordon was friendless and alone, we thought. Everyone we spoke to, who had any contact with him, spoke of him in the same way. Such an unpopular man, and yet so gentle and loving to the cats.

They were lessening in number, one or two having died and others strayed away, perhaps from whence they came originally. Gordon's own cat, Coco, however, was always beside him; sleeping on his bed, or rubbing herself against his grubby trouser legs, leaving black fur sticking to the rough material like a fell.

I personally had virtually no contact with Gordon these days. Just occasionally I answered a phone call when he was ringing Brian about some bill or other, and we exchanged civil pleasantries but little else. He never enquired after any of us… simply complained about his own situation; his health was poor and a varicose ulcer on his leg had necessitated a regular visit from a district nurse to dress it. These nurses rarely came more than once. I understand Gordon attacked one with his stick and left her bruised. Others complained about his appalling verbal abuse, especially if they were black girls. Male nurses were sent in the hopes that they might have more success, but in general Gordon found them distasteful as well, stating that no self-respecting male would take up nursing as a career as it was a menial task fit only for the lesser sex. This did not, with my nursing background, endear the fellow to me!

I was, however, affected by Brian's pity for him. Such a kind and caring man himself, Brian seemed able to overlook the terrible behaviour and things Gordon had done to make us feel so aggrieved in the past. He was confronted now by a pitiful old man, apparently alone in the world, and living in virtual squalor with a few mangy cats. Gone was the loving care administered so dutifully by Aunt Helen; the gentle coat brushing, attention to eyes, ears and teeth, and careful grooming to remove fur balls and burrs. Now the cats appeared fed but otherwise neglected, due in part to the fact that Gordon was now old and ill, and unable to venture downstairs to tend the cats in the main part of the house.

Brian found stinking cat litter on a number of occasions, and emptied the trays when he called. Mostly the cats avoided the trays now anyway, and left little 'parcels' and strong-smelling puddles anywhere and everywhere. Sometimes their food dishes were crawling with flies... we suspected that Gordon never washed them, and simply emptied new food from the tins into overused bowls.

'I can't bear to see him like this Mags,' Brian said one wintry evening after a routine visit to Elmwood.

'I've spent a couple of hours tonight just going through that huge heap of papers we brought from next door, and the old boy has done absolutely nothing for years. There were unpresented cheques so out of date they're no longer valid, and he just didn't care.'

'God, we'd care,' I said. Times were hard for us, having invested most of our savings in Andrew's new business to help him on his way. The venture looked so good and viable at first, but unforeseen circumstances were dramatically changing the outlook for the business and we were desperately worried.

Brian lay down an enormous pile of papers on the carpet, and dust flew out around them.

'Oh no, Bri, they're filthy! Must they come back here?'

'Well, I'd rather sort them at home than at Elmwood, to be honest. It's so terrible there and I almost have to hold my breath.'

He dusted the top of the pile with his handkerchief and pulled a face at the dirt.

'Sorry, love. I'll get a rubbish sack.'

I yawned, tired from my day looking after little Emily and her new baby sister Lauren. I was shortening a little dress for one of them and the stitches were beginning to blur as my eyes grew tired.

'Could you put the main light on, please, darling? I can't see well enough with just the lamp,' I asked, as Brian returned with a sack for the papers to be discarded. His mind was still at Elmwood; his brow furrowed as he worked through the pile.

'I don't see how he can go on living there you know,' he said, referring to Gordon's situation again. 'It's so unhygienic, and he can't cope on his own. I mentioned his son to him tonight, but there's no love lost there. I don't think they've been in touch for years and years... he doesn't even know where Paul is living.'

'That's odd, isn't it?' My interest was roused. I threaded my needle with fresh cotton.

'What did he say about Paul? Is he married, has he any children, that sort of thing? I never remember Gordon mentioning him at all.'

'Well no, it was always a taboo subject, wasn't it? Aunt Helen implied he was a useless son and that they'd been estranged for ages. I gather he was close to his mother, and when she died things fell apart completely between Gordon and Paul.'

'How sad now, to be in Gordon's state and to have no contact at all with your only son. Isn't that awful? Imagine if it was one of us and we didn't know where in the world Andrew or James were, or Lucy, for heaven's sake. I just can't contemplate it.'

'Fortunately you don't have to, darling. But you see why I feel so sorry for Gordon, don't you? He's still a cantankerous old devil, but he's a pitiful case, believe me.'

I put my sewing away wistfully, treasuring thoughts of my own children and little grandchildren, and felt deeply sad for Gordon, with virtually no one in the world to care about him, or, now that Aunt Helen was gone, for him to care about in return.

I began to bake cakes again for Gordon, and sent them to Elmwood whenever Brian went, on strict instructions that the tins in which they were sent were brought home immediately. I couldn't help remembering the fungal mould I had scrubbed out of Aunt Helen's cake tins in the pantry years before.

Having asked Brian to be his executor, Gordon wanted him to help him draw up a new will. His friend Wallace Beasby had died, and a 'young ruffian', as Gordon called him, had taken his place at the solicitor's office in Barnes.

'So what are we to do?' Brian asked one afternoon, sitting with Gordon in the upstairs kitchen, eating my lemon sponge and drinking tea from a well-scoured mug. Coco the cat was purring on his knee, and Gordon was smoking his pipe and sighing heavily.

'Well, I want to get a representative in from the Charity Aid Foundation,' he said, 'to give me advice about a new will. The old one just states that my estate is to go to the RSPCA.'

'What about your son Paul?'

'Hmph! Certainly not! He's no son of mine!'

Brian decided not to pursue the point, and he arranged for a lady from the Charity Aid Foundation to call in a fortnight's time.

The poor unsuspecting soul came on a Thursday afternoon, and Brian took some time out from his office to be at Elmwood to meet her with Gordon.

Mrs Briggs was a lady in late middle age, dressed in a smart navy suit, and clearly concerned about where to sit that would leave the least marks on her dark skirt. She smiled warmly at Gordon, who refused to shake her hand and simply grunted at her.

Mrs Briggs fingered her string of pink pearls nervously and Brian suppressed a smirk.

Gordon explained his wishes for a new will, and Mrs Briggs responded keenly, though clearly unaware of the amount the estate would raise.

'I'll send you some forms,' she said, making notes in a black plastic folder with a clipboard and pad on one side. She folded it over and returned it to her carrier bag, aptly decorated with rows of smiling cats.

'You'll need to fill them in and return them to me, and then we can proceed.'

Gordon nodded with his usual sigh. Absolutely everything now seemed to be a huge effort for him.

'Once that's done, I assume I can instruct a solicitor to draw up a new will,' he said. 'I don't want this wretched government to benefit from my money.'

He mumbled on and Brian took Mrs Briggs downstairs to see her out, amused to see her hurrying out of the gate at the end of the drive as though Satan himself was behind her.

Gordon's health declined and his situation at Elmwood worsened. Meals on Wheels were delivered; Brian had brought in shopping on a weekly basis for him for some time previously, but the time came when even heating up a ready meal was too much effort for the old man.

That year became increasingly busy for us at home, with two weddings to arrange; Andrew's to Mary, and Lucy's just six weeks later, to Daniel. Two new members of the family, and we loved them both. Our awareness of Gordon remained of course, and Brian fitted in his now regular visits as usual, but as the wedding dates came closer and our excitement increased we had more in mind to be concerned about.

The summer arrived in a flurry of invitations, maps to be produced of routes to reception venues, clothes to be planned and purchased, altered to fit, and shoes found to match.

Emily and Lauren, aged four and two, were to be bridesmaids for Lucy that October. Lucy herself was a bridesmaid for Mary, at Andrew's wedding in August. Our house was awash with gorgeous dresses on hangers suspended from picture rails, so as not to crush them, and shrouded in polythene wraps to keep them spotless.

Elmwood, and its squalor of the present day, was a far cry from the excitement within our home.

Lucy and I were sitting at the table in the dining room, making lists. Plans were well underway for Andrew's and Mary's wedding; in fact the parts for which we were responsible were already organised and we felt we were well on course for their big day in August. That left the arrangements to be finalised for October, and Lucy and Daniel had very definite ideas about that.

We sipped coffee as we checked our lists and I tried hard to separate the two weddings in my mind so as not to become confused. Lucy's hair, newly highlighted, flopped over one eye. She was growing it, and it was at the in-between stage. Her diamond engagement ring sparkled in the light from the lamp on the sideboard.

'George! Why must you lie right on my feet?' She leant over to adjust a dog; we now had two in the wake of dear old Cider, who had died some years before aged fifteen... not a bad age for a dog.

George and Millie were to be found wherever we were; on our feet under the table, on our knees in the sitting room, or under Brian's desk in his office, curled up beside him as he worked. When I was cooking in the kitchen they could be found at my feet waiting in quiet anticipation of dropped morsels.

'Do you think these two could be at the wedding wearing white ribbons?' Lucy suggested, jokingly, though I sensed there was an element of seriousness in her comment.

I laughed.

'Only if you really want there to be chaos,' I said. 'Although I somehow feel there will be chaos anyway, the way we're going on this guest list. Come on now, let's start this one again.'

Both weddings were wonderful; entirely happy, sunshine-filled days, and Brian and I shared a sense of total pleasure on seeing all our three dear children happily married to partners we loved. Our little granddaughters were enchanting bridesmaids; Emily with a cascade of brown curls and Lauren with her baby blonde ones, as they carried their little baskets of autumnal flame and gold flowers down the aisle behind Auntie Lucy, whom they adored.

Such happy days, such a loving and happy family. We all missed the dear grandparents; Brian's father, the last surviving one, having died in January at the great age of ninety-three. He had already met and become well acquainted with Mary as she and Andrew had been engaged for two years; and Lucy was glad that he had met Daniel too, just before he died, and declared him to be a 'nice young man.' Auntie Pearl was also missing from the celebrations; she had died the previous year, having lived near us in Ealing in a residential home for the last year of her life. Lucy especially, was close to Auntie Pearl, and would like her to have known Daniel.

'She'd have loved him, darling,' I remember saying. 'Just her type. They'd have got on like a house on fire.'

'She wouldn't have seen him, though Mum, being blind… she wouldn't have known how handsome he is.' Lucy sighed.

It was so good to see her so happy and in love.

Their wedding celebrations lasted into the night and Brian and I were almost the last to leave. As we flopped wearily into our car at the main door of the hotel, just a handful of young people remained in the riverside bar, overlooking Chelsea Harbour.

'What's the time?' I yawned, manoeuvring myself carefully into the passenger seat beneath Lucy's bouquet and the bridesmaids' posies and baskets of flowers. The back of the car was full of wonderful presents, flower arrangements from the church and the reception tables, and heaven knows what else that was essential to keep.

Brian loosened his morning suit tie, suitably gold in colour and fashionably 'scrunched'. He too yawned, and started the engine for our hour's drive home.

'One a.m.,' he said wearily but happily. 'It all went so well, didn't it?'

I smiled.

'Really well, darling. Everything was wonderful.'

'And I didn't make too much of a pig's ear of my speech?'

'Never. It was fantastic, just as I knew it would be. You are perfection on legs, and if I could lean over and kiss you I would, but all these flowers prevent me.'

'Steady on, old girl, none of that! I'm driving, under duress. Can't see much out of the rear window actually...'

The roads through London were clear and the autumn night crisp. We were glad to see James in his pyjamas waiting for us as we pulled into the drive, ready to help us offload. The house was full of people; family who had descended on us for the wedding from all over the place, but everyone was silently sleeping as we crept into the hall at two o'clock in the morning.

'I waited up to give you a hand,' James said quietly, humping a large flower arrangement through the front door and dislodging tall stems of greenery. 'We've only just got Emily off to sleep, she was still buzzing with all the excitement.'

'And Lauren, bless her? Is she OK?'

'Absolutely fine. Slept all the way back in the car and didn't even stir when we undressed her.'

'Cup of tea?' Brian asked, but we both declined and opted for bed.

James turned on the stairs, suddenly remembering something.

'Oh, Dad... there's a cranky message for you on the answerphone. I can't make it out; long silences and mumbles. You might want to listen.'

I had already flicked the switch to replay, and a faint and feeble voice came over, simply calling Brian. I turned up the volume, hoping not to disturb the sleepers upstairs, but no one stirred.

'Brian?...' again. And again, then nothing, but the receiver at the other end was not replaced.

Brian, listening beside me, sighed heavily.

'It's Gordon,' we said together.

'I can't deal with it now, love,' Brian said wearily. 'First thing in the morning though. Can't do anything at this time of night. Let's get to bed.'

We fell under the duvet, contented with the wedding, but concerned about Gordon, and slept.

The bedside clock said six a.m., and I realised that I had been woken by the phone bell, ringing shrilly in the quiet house. Brian was shouting into the receiver beside the bed.

'OK, Gordon, yes, I'm here. Right... I'm coming over... I'll be with you very soon.'

I sat upright, yawning myself awake.

'No, Bri, you're surely not going to Barnes now... it's only six o'clock.'

He was pulling on his socks and dressing with urgency, his face still creased with sleep.

Little Emily padded into our room, rubbing her eyes, her beloved Bagpuss under her arm. Silently, she climbed into bed beside me and snuggled into the crook of my arm, settling herself to sleep again as small, exhausted bridesmaids do.

Brian whispered so as not to disturb her, as he pulled on a jumper, discarded on the chair the previous morning.

'Darling, I must. Gordon's on the floor. He fell yesterday and couldn't get up, and he couldn't reach us on the phone because we were all at the wedding. He's been there ever since, and he sounds terrible. Heaven knows what I'm going to find.'

'Oh Bri... and I can't come with you and leave everyone here... we've got the lunch party this morning. Hell... wouldn't you just know it!'

He planted a hasty kiss on my forehead as he hurried out with a brief 'See you as soon as I can', and I heard the car engine hum into action moments later as he drove away.

Friends and family joined us throughout the morning, and I gratefully left Andrew and James to welcome everyone with drinks in Brian's stead, while I prepared salads in the kitchen with the girls. Mary kept the kettle boiling for those who needed coffee. She looked so happy, having only recently returned with Andrew from their honeymoon in Thailand, and she was re-living their own happy day again as we celebrated Lucy's and Daniel's.

Eventually Brian returned, having called an ambulance for Gordon and sorted out the disasters of the previous day and night. Gordon, however, had refused to leave the house, so a hospital stay to recover was not in order, and having lifted all six foot of him back into bed, the ambulance crew left him in Brian's care.

'I told him I couldn't stay,' Brian said, recounting the events of the past few hours to me in the kitchen. He nibbled biscuits in lieu of breakfast, and leant on the work surface while I piped cream on a trifle.

'He was clearly miffed, but very tired, and in quite a bit of pain really, having been stuck lying on a cold hard floor for so long. I gave him some aspirin and a mug of coffee, and left him a tray of lunch by the bed. Very grudgingly, he said he'd manage.'

Lesley appeared in the kitchen with a tray of glasses, the sound of laughter and voices of all descriptions following her loudly through the door. Little Lauren was wrapped around her leg, sucking a thumb.

'Lauren wants to be with Granny,' Lesley announced. 'Too many big people in there, I think. Is it okay if I leave her with you?'

Brian scooped Lauren up and tickled her, grinning at her infectious toddler chuckle. She stroked the top of his head.

'Grandpa, you haven't any hair on here,' she commented, investigating the bald area.

We all laughed, and I mused thankfully on the way small children can totally alter one's mood from concern to delight in a split second.

We enjoyed the rest of the wedding weekend to the full, resolving to sort Gordon's situation out once the celebrations were over.

Chapter Nine

A late Indian summer had been perfect for us that year, creeping as it did into early October, to warm us with its sunshine for Lucy's wedding. Andrew and Mary, returning from their honeymoon, had commented that it was almost as warm in England as it had been on their idyllic island of Phuket. They made a striking couple, both tall, and complementing one another as they did; he with darker hair and she blonde.

Mary was a psychiatric nurse, calm and gentle, reassuring and kind. We were eternally thankful for her loving support of Andrew when almost at once on their return home, his business hit rock bottom and he struggled to keep it going against all odds. Brian put more money in, hoping it might serve to resurrect the company, but I was very afraid for the future of us all.

One November evening, cool but clear, Brian drove as usual to Elmwood with provisions for Gordon, and a sheaf of papers to be dealt with. The forms promised by Mrs Briggs of the Charity Aid Foundation were long since overdue, and without completion of these, Gordon's new will could not be drawn up.

I expected Brian to be late home, so I kept some cottage pie warm in the oven for his return. The key turned in the door, and both dogs ran to greet him.

'Hey, you're home earlier than I thought you'd be,' I called, lighting the gas under the vegetable saucepan. He appeared in the kitchen for his welcome home kiss.

'You won't believe this, Mags,' he said, removing his fleece. 'When I arrived at Elmwood, I used my key as usual, and all the downstairs was dark.'

Gordon was virtually bedridden now, and the nursing team who bravely attended him had been given a key.

'I went on up as usual, and heard voices, so I thought it must be the TV... you know how loud Gordon has it, he's so deaf now.'

We settled at the kitchen table to have a glass of wine while we waited for the broccoli to cook.

'Well,' Brian continued, obviously enjoying telling his tale, 'when I went along the landing, I called out as usual to tell Gordon I'd arrived, and out of his room came the oddest bloke… I had quite a shock, I can tell you!'

'Who was he? Did you know him?'

'Not likely; he's a scruffy fellow, unshaven and skinny, but with a nice smile. He said he's Trevor Hill, and he used to do odd gardening jobs for Aunt Helen, apparently.'

I knew that there had been a chap years ago, who came twice a year for a week at a time, to 'wake the garden up in the spring, and put it to bed in the autumn,' as Aunt Helen had said. Not the regular gardener, but a fly-by-night who appeared each March and October, and was then gone again as fast as he had come. I supposed this must be the same man, but I didn't think he had been to Elmwood for some years.

'Well,' Brian went on, 'he told me that he has moved in to Elmwood for the time being at Gordon's request to give him a hand; you know, answering the door to the Meals on Wheels people, and so forth. He's made a room for himself on the top floor and he seems quite cosy, but actually, Gordon isn't at all comfortable with the idea.'

'That's very odd, if he asked this Trevor to move in, like you said?'

I served the cottage pie and broccoli, steaming, onto plates at the table, and we ate.

'Well, that's what I thought,' said Brian, between mouthfuls. The dogs arrived at our feet, quietly hoping for leftovers.

'But although Gordon was his usual grumpy self when we were alone; muttering and complaining about Trevor; it doesn't mean he didn't ask him. I must admit, it seems like a useful idea, if he's all above board, so to speak, because he can do shopping and so forth, and make a big difference to Gordon on a daily basis. In return for his keep, I suppose,' he added.

'Doesn't he have a home then, or a job?' I asked.

Brian shook his head, his mouth full.

'Seems not. If he hadn't said, I'd have thought from the look of him that he'd been sleeping under Barnes Bridge. He told me he's 'invalided-out' of work with a bad back, and he's 'in-between' houses at the moment.'

'Hmph! Sounds a bit odd to me. I hope he isn't up to no good, Bri… there are all those lovely antiques there, and all Aunt Helen's jewellery that Gordon won't have touched!'

'Yes, I know, I thought of that too. But quite honestly, everything is so filthy now, no one would want to root around in the cupboards. Anyway, old Gordon's still very astute, and he's always there. Trevor will just be around to feed the cats, and get breakfast and things. I'm pretty sure it's all okay.'

We cleared the plates and took bowls of apple crumble into the sitting room in order to watch the television news. I felt a twinge of apprehension about Trevor Hill, and wondered if I should ever meet him. Perhaps he would disappear as quickly as he had come, bearing the brunt of Gordon's displeasure at some tiny misdemeanour or other.

Not so. Christmas was on the horizon, and the weather worsened. Trevor Hill, apparently homeless, remained at Elmwood, despite frequent unpleasant arguments with Gordon over trivial things. They seemed to be a sad pair, but settled together they were, living at arm's length with one another in the utter squalor that was Elmwood. I felt Trevor must have been a very sorry case to have nowhere more amiable to live than there, amongst the filth and stench, and with only Gordon's vile temper for company.

I made them a Christmas cake, and Brian drove it over the week before Christmas. He found Gordon in a sorry state, totally unable to get up or dressed, and coughing piteously.

Trevor was noticeable by his absence, and when Brian enquired as to his whereabouts, Gordon waved one hand dismissively and scowled.

'Bah! I neither know nor care where the scoundrel is,' he gasped, triggering another bout of coughing.

'Sometimes he's here, sometimes not, but he never tells me where or when he's going. Look at that, will you!' (indicating the window at the end of the bed); 'I told him to pull the curtains for me and he's only done one of the wretched things!'

Brian rectified the curtain, noticing a broken window pane through which blew a blast of cold, pre-Christmas air, with an icy nip to it.

'No wonder your chest's bad, Gordon,' he said. 'You're in a heck of a draught from this window.'

He fetched some thick cardboard from a heap of unsorted rubbish downstairs, and taped it over the pane, sadness in his heart that his uncle's once beautiful house had come to this.

I was wrapping Christmas stocking oddments on the sitting room floor when he came home, and he crouched beside me, pressing a finger on a parcel while I cut the Sellotape.

'He's not so good tonight, Mags,' he said. 'Coughing and spluttering like a trooper. His cheeks were flushed, too.'

'He's got a fever, I dare say,' I mumbled, with tape between my teeth. 'Ought he to see the doctor, would you say? If so, we ought to phone in the morning, because next week will be hectic in the surgery before Christmas. Is he really bad?'

Brian shrugged.

'I can't tell, really. You'd know more than me. But a doctor's visit couldn't hurt, and he is over ninety.'

'Tomorrow, then. Well actually, why not ask Trevor to phone, and then he'll be there to open the door to the doctor?'

'I don't know where he was tonight,' said Brian. 'It's funny; I always feel he could up and leave at any time and we'd never know; Gordon doesn't ever know when he's going out it seems. They'd fallen out this evening over his curtains,' he added with a smile.

I have always loved Christmas, and the presence of children makes it perfect. Christmas stockings for Emily and Lauren, complete with mince pies and carrots on the front step for Father Christmas and his reindeer. Church on Christmas morning, surrounded by my family to welcome Jesus's birth, and a giant turkey roasting slowly, all night long; the dogs' little noses twitching in the kitchen as they dozed in their baskets.

Twinkling lights on the Christmas tree, decorations and literally hundreds of cards all over the house, and piles of exciting presents for everyone, wrapped in colourful paper with shiny ribbons.

What a contrast it would be, I thought, for Gordon and possibly Trevor, if he remained there long enough, spending a miserable and lonely Christmas at Elmwood.

It was not, however, to be. Trevor telephoned on Christmas Eve to tell us that he had called the doctor for the second time, and Gordon had been taken into hospital with a chest infection. Sorry as I was for him, it was obviously the best place for him to be, and I grinned to myself as I thought of the problems the nurses were going to have with such a cantankerous old man.

Christmas came and went in a flurry; a thin white dusting of snow, decorating the garden and the pavements as we woke on Christmas morning. Two excited little girls checked the front step for reindeer hoof prints, and instead discovered an empty mince pie plate and a half eaten carrot as evidence of a special visit in the night.

The excitement of family parties, presents and festivities soon over, we took down the decorations and the tree, and packed away the baubles and the tinsel in the old paraffin heater box, labelled in my dear old Dad's handwriting: 'Xmas Decos.'

New Year's Day left me wondering what the year ahead would bring. Andrew's business at the gym in Wimbledon, was sinking fast, and was sadly therefore, up for sale. We were all so very much aware of the loss of so much money for each of us, and in order to keep the gym open to obtain a purchaser, yet more finance dribbled away like sand through our fingers every week. I ached as I watched my darling Brian drained and worried, working so hard for so little, and with such enormous losses ahead. I was also very afraid for Andrew and Mary, and panic hit me often in the night, as Brian slept fitfully beside me.

Gordon never returned to Elmwood.

Early in January, his chest infection worsened into pneumonia, and one cold winter evening we heard over the telephone that he had died.

That, really, was when it all finally began.

Chapter Ten

That January was a bad one; the weather poor even for the time of year, and life in general, for us, was worrying and hard. I was increasingly concerned for Brian, whose plate seemed to be constantly full of work, other people's troubles, and because of our financial situation, fears for our future and Andrew's and Mary's as well. And on top of all this, there was Gordon's estate to deal with now, and the funeral to arrange.

'Bri, what about that son?' I mentioned over our coffee, following the phone call to tell us that Gordon had died. 'Surely we ought to contact him... he'll need to know.'

'Well, I don't know where he is at all,' Brian said. 'But you're right; we need to locate him somehow and tell him the news.'

The wind howled outside and the two dogs left their position at the window, where they were on evening 'fox-watch', and curled up together in front of the fire.

'Perhaps he will want to be involved in the funeral plans,' I went on, still thinking of Paul Lench.

'I very much doubt it, somehow.'

Brian pressed the remote control for the News at Ten coverage on the television.

'He hasn't been in touch for years, by all accounts. No love lost between them... very sad state of affairs.'

'Couldn't you find a phone number for him in the house somewhere? In an old address book, maybe?'

'I'll have a look tomorrow. I need to take a day off to deal with everything really; fetching the death certificate from the hospital, and registering the death and so on. Then I'll go to Elmwood and hunt out a number for Paul. There's a chance, of course, that if there is one, it will be so old by now that he's moved on, but we must try.'

Surprisingly, this job was taken out of our hands by Trevor Hill. When we arrived at Elmwood the following lunchtime (I had gone with Brian to help where possible) Trevor met us in the hall, looking every bit the 'down-and-out' I had been led to expect. He was unshaven, thin and pale, and he wore navy corduroy trousers covered in stains and worn patches. It was difficult to tell his age, but I supposed he was younger than he looked, probably in his forties.

Brian introduced me, and as Trevor shook my hand, I noticed that he had filthy nails, and crooked yellow teeth but a warm smile.

'I've spoken to Gordon's son Paul,' he said, addressing Brian rather than me. 'I found an old address and phone book with his number in from years ago, but he's still at that address so I got hold of him, no trouble.'

'Oh, well thank you, Trevor.' Brian seemed unsure as to whether this had been a good idea or otherwise. I wondered how Trevor had introduced himself; 'I'm a squatter in the house your father's been living in for the past eight years,' perhaps?

'I'll phone Paul tonight, if you'll give me that number. Maggie and I are here to dig out necessary forms. We need a birth certificate for Gordon and so on, in order to register his death.'

Trevor gave a knowing smile, and I felt decidedly unnerved.

'You'll find everything you need in his desk,' he told us, indicating the room upstairs which had once been Malcolm's bedroom. Obviously, since Trevor had moved into the house some two months previously, he had spent plenty of time rooting about in drawers and cupboards, and he was now well acquainted with probably everything private and personal of not only Gordon, but Aunt Helen as well, from many years previously. Since her death, nothing had been cleared at all, other than the dirty bed linen which I disposed of myself. Otherwise, her belongings had remained untouched by anyone, fiercely protected by Gordon at all times.

Brian noticed that Uncle Tom's old study, previously always kept locked, was now open, the door ajar into the hallway. I peered inside. Once elegant furnishings were covered with a thick layer of grey dust. I wiped a finger along the mahogany desk, leaving a deep trail. The wallpaper was faded and peeling below the picture rail; obviously another damp wall affected by the urgent need for work to be done on the roof.

On one wall hung a collection of Uncle Tom's head attire over the years of his life, displayed interestingly in order, from his school caps through university sports' caps to a war beret and an officer's cap of the RAF. There was a university black mortar board complete with dangling tassel, a Sea Scout cap and a black bowler hat, probably from Uncle Tom's working days in central London at the Physical Science Institute. All were shrouded in a thick layer of dust, cobwebs connecting each item on the wall, and I suspected, spiders nesting in the crowns.

All over the walls were framed photographs; Uncle Tom at school as school captain, cricket captain and rugby captain, seated centrally in each picture, with rows and teams of boys around him. There were wartime photos of Uncle Tom in uniform, and several of Malcolm, aged between about seven and nineteen, looking quite the dapper young man of the fifties.

I browsed quietly in the study, hearing Brian and Trevor chatting in the hallway outside the door, but unaware of the details of their conversation.

A fly buzzed sleepily by the window pane, trying to find a way out without any luck. I realised that it must have come in through the now open hallway door, as the window had obviously remained firmly shut for goodness knows how many years. The curtains were partly closed, and their colour faded in stripes where they had been exposed to the sunshine for so long without movement.

All around the walls were shelves of books, stacks of files, and in one corner, a neat pile of very old leather attaché cases, the fabric of which was crumbling and cracked. Elsewhere on the floor were piles upon piles of folders, papers and document files, stashed high against one another; and under the window was a stack of old boxes, tied firmly with string, and covered in a deep layer of dust.

Brian poked his head around the door.

'Oh, you're still in here, Mags... my God, look at this!' He let out a slow, deep breath as he took in what he saw before him. 'I'm going to have to go through all this.'

'Unless someone else has done it before you,' I whispered, wondering whether Trevor was within earshot.

Brian smiled, understanding my meaning, and raised his eyebrows.

It felt very strange to think that this lay-about individual had total access to all the family details, in a house which didn't in any way belong to him.

With that, Trevor called from upstairs, asking whether we would like tea as the kettle had boiled.

'Thanks, yes, I think so,' Brian answered.

'We'll be a while hunting out the things we need.'

I shook my head at him, frowning.

'Don't think I could stomach it,' I whispered, and he grinned.

'Just do your best,' he mocked.

We joined Trevor in the upstairs kitchen, where I noticed quite a transformation had occurred.

'You've had a sort-out, Trevor,' I said, indicating the now neat piles of old newspapers, letters and paperwork on the table, instead of the appalling mess that had once been Gordon's.

Coco the cat purred round my ankles.

'She's the reason I'm still here,' Trevor said, stroking her black fur. 'She and the other cats, of course. Old Gordon asked me to stay and look after them when he went into hospital three weeks ago. Can't leave now, can I?' One corner of his mouth turned up in a sneakily questioning smile.

Brian, stirring his tea in a relatively clean-looking mug, gave an uneasy cough.

'Trevor, we'll have to see about that,' he said. 'The house officially belongs to the Cats' Charity you see.' And he went on to explain to Trevor about the old agreement for Gordon to stay over the years. Trevor, however, appeared to be well aware of the situation, and already had a plan to keep himself secure in his shabby accommodation on the top floor.

'I'm just honouring the old man's wishes,' he said, but we wondered whether this was at all true.

'Can't leave, while the cats are still here. Especially Coco, eh, my lovely? This is her home… wouldn't do to uproot her, would it now?' He petted the cat gently, and she jumped onto his knee, purring loudly.

'How many others are left, Trevor?' I asked, aware that Coco was the only cat to be seen indoors.

'Oh, now...' he scratched his whiskery beard as if counting in his head. 'Five or six, if you count the strays that come and go in the shelters. I have to feed them outside, of course, and then there are the three indoors.'

'Three?'

'There's Coco here, and Tuppeny and Smokey, the big fellow...'

I listened with interest, as these were names of old cats in Aunt Helen's time, now definitely lying in state in marked garden graves.

When we had finished our tea... I managed to drink very little, but so as not to give offence I poured it surreptitiously down the sink when Trevor wasn't looking... we went around the rooms one by one. The only room we didn't enter was the bedroom on the top floor where Trevor had taken up residence, and I noticed his door was firmly shut. What, I wondered, was he hiding in there? What sort of living conditions had he accepted, in this horrendously dirty house? It remained a mystery.

All the other rooms without exception were in an appalling state given that no one had cleaned any of them in any way for at least nine years. The once beautiful carpets were littered with cat faeces; many now white with age. In Gordon's bedroom the ceiling had come down with damp at one time, and been shoddily repaired but no renovations done to the ruined décor and the cracked, stained walls. Wallpaper hung in huge folds where it had come away from the plaster. The curtains were so dirty that I suspected they would fall to pieces if they were taken down and washed. The bed linen, left on since the night Gordon was taken to hospital and untouched for three weeks, was disgusting. I suspected that it had not been changed for months before that, and there was a rank odour as we entered the room. I vowed to bundle it into a bin liner and throw it away, along with the horribly stained pillows and blankets, which smelt vile, even at a distance.

Evidence was everywhere of an old man who years ago had lost all self-respect, and to whom the word hygiene had come to mean nothing at all.

Aunt Helen's room was equally shocking, and Malcolm's old bedroom, turned into Gordon's study when he moved in many years ago, another example of dirt and degradation. Amazingly, an old vacuum cleaner leant against the wall, so old and out of date that I wondered whether it would explode if we were to switch it on. It had clearly not been moved or used for over ten years, but the dust bag was bursting at the seams with even older filth. When, I wondered to myself, was that last emptied?

The longer we remained, the more the stench of cats' excrement clung in my nostrils. I understood why Brian had hated his regular visits so much, and admired him for his kindness and constancy in helping Gordon when there was no one else to care.

We drove home disconsolate, and Brian's responsibilities surrounding Elmwood seemed to be increasing by the day.

'I'm concerned about Trevor, Mags,' he said, rounding the bend of the lane by the river, and joining a stream of early evening traffic returning home from work.

'I sort of fear he's going to put up opposition to moving out when the Cats' Charity asks him to leave the house. What do you think?'

'Well, I thought the same. He seems so settled, somehow, and what was all that about extra cats? Do you suppose he's inventing them, in order to have a reason to stay?'

'Hmm, I did wonder. He's even calling them the names from the little graves outside.'

'Sounds like he wants to stay, to me,' I said, thoughtfully. 'Though who on earth would actually want to remain in all that squalor I can't imagine, not in their right mind, anyway. He's certainly an oddball, that one.'

We hit the traffic lights by the brewery, and Brian sighed, tired from a wearisome day. We just wanted to get home and shower to feel clean again.

'I'm also worried about all the valuables,' he said. 'If you think about it, there's all Aunt Helen's old jewellery somewhere there, and the silver and heaven knows, that's worth a bit.'

'What about Gordon's stuff? Anything valuable of his?'

Brian nodded.

'I don't know exactly, but I would expect there are a few things, certainly. And it's all at Trevor's disposal, isn't it? We don't know him from a bar of soap, really, so we can't say if he's trustworthy.'

The following morning, Brian telephoned Frank Willis at the

Cats' Charity, to make him aware of the situation.

'You may possibly have a job on your hands,' he told Frank, who was the solicitor now dealing with legacies, in place of Vic Towers whom we had met years ago.

'I rather feel that Trevor Hill may dig his heels in, in order to keep the roof over his head, though heaven only knows how he can stomach it there.'

'Hmm… maybe I should visit,' Frank suggested. 'Do a quick recce, so to speak, now that the house has finally come into our hands.'

'Good idea, but could you wait until after the funeral, and I could meet you there? I'm trying to arrange it for next week, so I'll be somewhat tied up until after that.'

'No problem. Phone me again when you're ready.'

We arranged Gordon's funeral for ten days' time, having spoken to his son Paul on the telephone. I made the call when Brian was out the following afternoon, and spoke to Paul's wife Linda at first. A friendly sounding soul, she explained that Paul, now sixty-eight, had recently been unwell.

'He's always suffered with his nerves,' she said, 'and he really doesn't like the telephone.'

Her voice faded as she obviously turned away from the receiver, addressing her husband in the background.

'She sounds like a nice lady, Paul; come and talk to her.'

A pause, and then:

'Well, she won't bite you, for heaven's sake! Just come here and speak to her for a moment. Hallo?'

Louder again, to me this time.

'Maggie? He won't take the phone… oh, here he is now.'

'Hallo, Maggie? Sorry for the delay… I—'

'Paul, hallo. It's good to speak to you. I'm really phoning for Brian, my husband, because we're trying to arrange your father's funeral.'

He cut me short.

'He's not my father! Never was… not in the true sense of the word. I'll not be coming, Maggie, to a funeral… you understand… we haven't seen the old man for over twenty years, and that visit was a mistake, I can tell you.'

'I'm very sorry, Paul, this must be hard for you,' I said gently. 'Of course we understand if you'd rather not come, but we do need your permission to go ahead with the arrangements. Is there any particular thing you'd like done?'

Silence for a while... I wondered if he'd gone. Then Linda returned.

'No, nothing, Maggie. Maybe we should have your phone number, if your husband is the executor, and he'll be dealing with things.'

I gave it to her, somewhat puzzled by the pair of them, we exchanged pleasantries, and I hung up. Odd, I thought, wondering with interest what could have happened in Paul's younger days to have caused such intense dislike of his father.

Brian surprised me on the Friday when I returned from Tesco's, with the news that Linda had phoned while I was out, and she and Paul would now be coming to the funeral. It was to be a cremation at Mortlake, and we feared there would be less than a small handful of people present.

He helped me to bring my shopping in from the car, running in his slippers, as it was raining heavily.

I unpacked chips and lamb steaks into the freezer, as Brian flicked the switch on the kettle to make tea.

'It was Linda who phoned,' he said, emptying the new milk carton into the jug from the fridge.

'Yes, it would be. She told me Paul doesn't like speaking to people; she said he suffers with his nerves, or something.'

'That's what she told me too. I dare say that's got something to do with his original decision not to come to the funeral. However, now they've changed their minds and they will be coming, and bringing some cousin or other, apparently.'

'Well, I'm glad there will be some family people there after all.'

We sat at the kitchen table for our tea, steaming in chunky mugs. I warmed my hands around mine, cold from my shopping trip in icy wind. The dogs had arrived to greet me from their respective sleeping places in basket and mat by the French windows... an observation point manned by them in turn on the lookout for foxes in the back garden. They sat at our feet, hoping for biscuits, as we opened a new packet of Hobnobs.

'It would be a sad thing to have no family or friends at your funeral,' Brian agreed, crunching. 'I would think we'll still be very few.'

'I'll be interested to meet Paul and Linda,' I mused.

As it happened, I had to wait longer than anticipated. Just before the funeral, Linda phoned again and informed us that their plans had changed once more, and the cousin would be attending without them.

'Paul can't do it after all,' she said quietly. 'He's not been well, you see, it would all be too much.'

'We understand, Linda, don't worry,' I reassured her. 'Funerals are difficult occasions; don't worry about it.'

'Oh... it's not like that, Maggie,' Linda explained.

'Paul wouldn't be upset, you know. He and old Gordon weren't at all close; more like daggers drawn, I'd say. No, it's just that he finds any sort of a 'do' a bit of a problem really.' She lowered her voice... 'He's never been confident, if you know what I mean.'

'Linda, did Paul have a bad time as a boy, with Gordon?' I asked, carefully. 'I get the impression that he didn't have a happy childhood, somehow. I don't mean to pry,' I added.

It was like opening the flood gates... Linda poured out the story as she knew it, obviously keen for me to understand how she felt about her father-in-law.

'You're so right, Maggie, he did not!' she said. 'That old bugger was cruelty itself, and Paul just a boy of sixteen when his mother died. Now they were close,' she added.

'A lovely lady, so I gather, was Florrie. She died suddenly, you know, and Paul was just bereft.'

'Maybe Gordon was too, Linda, and he just couldn't comfort his son,' I suggested.

'Huh! No, that wasn't the case at all. I think Gordon had never loved Paul; you know he was adopted just before the war; and when Florrie died it was an excuse not to go on bothering with the boy, as he called him.'

Linda sighed, and drew a long breath.

'Well, that's what I think, anyhow.'

'Poor Paul, Linda. I'm so sorry. We'll perfectly understand

about the funeral. I expect you'll hear about it, if you want to of course, from Paul's cousin, if she's there.'

'Oh, she will be, I'm sure. But we don't see much of her, actually, either...'

What a dysfunctional family, I thought, feeling so thankful for our own.

The day of the funeral was drab and cold, with a brisk easterly wind whipping around our legs as we waited at the crematorium for the previous service in the chapel to be over.

There were seven of us present; Brian and I, Louise, to lend support, Paul's cousin Jane and her daughter Vicky, and interestingly, Trevor Hill and Sam from Elmwood, who had arrived in a reasonable looking car belonging surprisingly to Trevor.

Gone for the day was the vagrant-like stubble and the scruffy clothes, and Trevor looked amazingly presentable.

Once the cremation was over... and no one shed a tear... we all went our separate ways. No tea and tiny sandwiches; or comforting remarks to one another to sympathise with or ease each other's grief. Just the biting wind and grey skies of a winter afternoon, causing our cheeks to glow in the cold. Petals from our wreath of yellow and white chrysanthemums blew along the damp pathway as it lay behind the chapel afterwards, a sign resting by it stating 'Gordon Lench', among so many others, for other people. Ours was the only one for him.

I read the little card I had written to attach to the wreath: 'Remembrance of a man who loved all birds and animals, from us, the Fawley family and especially his beloved cat Coco.' I had thought that Aunt Helen would have liked that.

We thanked the minister who had conducted the short ceremony so well, and had included the singing of 'All things bright and beautiful' at our request, because it appropriately mentioned birds and animals in its verses.

Standing at the end of the path, sheltering from the wind, was Gordon's niece Jane and her daughter, and we all exchanged introductions. Jane explained that they had all been out of touch with the old man for years, but that they used to send him a Christmas card.

'Just for old time's sake, you know,' she said. 'He and my father were brothers. I'm not surprised Paul didn't come. He's a very nervy chap, really, and doesn't like meeting people much.'

Very cautiously, Jane let us know that the family felt sorry for Paul; that his childhood and especially teenage years once his beloved mother had died, had been miserable at the hands of his father. I kept all these comments and gems of information stored in my memory, interested as I now was to discover the real story of Gordon Lench and his involvement in Elmwood.

It was beginning to take shape... horribly.

Chapter Eleven

Frank Willis arrived to see Elmwood the following week, wearing a forest green body warmer to keep out the winter chill. We were both at the house to meet him, and Brian suggested tea later, at a coffee shop by Barnes pond. This avoided us staying any longer than necessary at the house in the putrid atmosphere, or in the company of Trevor Hill. Frank was clearly relieved at the suggestion, and we walked together, leaning into the strong, cold wind.

As we passed 'number one', Belinda Morris and her two daughters were offloading shopping from her car, and I realised from a quick glance that both little girls had chickenpox, so I stopped to chat and commiserate. Brian and Frank walked ahead, hands in pockets, and I called that I would catch them up.

'Oh, deary me, I can see what you two have been up to,' I smiled.

Two little faces, covered in the various stages of the chicken-pox rash, grinned back.

Belinda sighed wearily.

'They've not been too bad,' she said.

'It looks worse than they've felt, I think. The difficult thing is having to leave them in the car at the shops. I didn't think Sainsbury's would be too pleased if they came inside with me. They should be back to school at the end of next week. With luck,' she added.

'I remember all this so well,' I sympathised. 'It's dreadful when they are ill, isn't it?'

Belinda nodded with feeling, and the girls began to squabble about which video they would watch indoors.

'I'll leave you to it,' I added, and hurried on to join the men, who were rounding the corner of the lane towards the pond, and the very nice little tea shop, which sold home-made scones.

As soon as we arrived, we went to wash in turns in the pretty toilet for customers' use, where there were fresh flowers on the windowsill in a blue china jug, and even hand cream for patrons to enjoy after washing. A far cry, I thought, from the filthy washbasin, grubby soap and downright dirty towel in the cloakroom at Elmwood. I made a mental note to replace the latter on our next visit, and to bring rubber gloves and scouring equipment too.

We ordered tea and a plate of home-made scones, which arrived with thick cream and raspberry jam in little pots.

Frank was friendly and warm. He was obviously shocked by the situation he was now having to deal with, and more than a little taken aback by Trevor Hill's determined effort to remain in place at Elmwood.

'I've explained to the fellow that he has to leave now,' Frank said, spreading his scone with jam. He declined the cream.

'But I have to say I met with quite considerable resistance. He gave me a load of stuff about feeding the cats, of course.'

'I said he would,' mumbled Brian, with his mouth full.

'… and I explained that we'll have them re-homed and well cared for. That's when he hit the roof and shouted that it was contrary to the last wishes of an old man, and before that Lady Helen.'

'Poppycock! It's a ruse to stay in the house with a roof over his head, I'd say.' Brian was indignant, and I had to agree.

'What happens next, Frank, if he refuses to go?' I asked.

'We'll give him several warnings, and if after a while he's still there we'll serve an eviction order.'

He added a considerable amount of milk to his tea and gulped it down quickly. 'Though it's something I hate doing, I'll admit. Much rather he went on his way of his own accord.'

I poured us all a second cup, and the waitress brought us more hot water for the pot.

'Frank, do you have to deal with things like this often, at the charity?' I asked, and he nodded, brushing crumbs from the patterned jumper he wore under his body warmer.

'Oh yes, I'm afraid so, now and again. Or equivalent problems relating to relatives who feel they are suffering injustice, because the charity is benefiting from a will instead of them. We have lots of those.'

'So you do have a lot of old ladies leaving you their fortunes?'

'Most certainly; I believe more old ladies, and quite a few old gents as well, leave their estates to the cats than to any other charity. It keeps me busy, I can tell you.'

Frank's smile was warm, and his face open and honest. I liked him, and felt he would deal fairly with Trevor and the situation at Elmwood. Brian was finding it all quite difficult, struggling as we were with our own dwindling finances, and already heavily in debt owing to the support we had given to Andrew's gym.

Brian paid the bill for our tea and we left, walking different ways to our separate cars. Frank and Brian had agreed to talk soon on the phone, when Trevor had been given a few days to clear himself and his belongings out of the house.

'I wonder how many of Gordon's and Aunt Helen's things will leave Elmwood with him?' I pondered, hooking my arm through Brian's as we walked back past the pond. A pair of mallards were huddled together in the bushes at the side, nestling to keep the cold from rustling their feathers.

Grey clouds scudded overhead, and two children, well wrapped in woollen hats and mufflers, arrived with a bag of bread to feed the ducks. Their young mother manipulated a buggy in which howled a toddler, red in the face with the cold, but kicking his pram rug away from his chubby legs in rage.

'Look, Martin, if you don't stop screaming, we won't have McDonald's for tea!' she pleaded, but as we walked by it seemed as if her efforts were in vain. Martin's screams grew louder, and we hurried past.

Our car was parked at the end of Elmwood's drive, and as we reached it I noticed Trevor Hill at the front door of the house, armed with a large mallet and some planks of wood.

I dug Brian in the ribs.

'Look Bri! What's he doing?'

'Good Lord; looks like he's boarding the place up! You stay here in the car; I'm going to have a word.'

He strode off down the drive, and I watched from the car at the gate.

At a distance I could just make out a large paper or card sign which was taped over the glass in the door, but it was impossible to see what was written on it. Trevor and Brian had an apparently amicable conversation, and he returned to the car, shaking his head in disbelief.

'You'd never credit it,' he said, starting the engine and driving away at speed.

'The guy just has to be crazy. He's boarding up the door, apparently to anyone except me, and there's a huge sign to say so on the glass panel. I tried to read it, but it's a load of garbage, Mags… doesn't make sense at all.'

'In what way? What does it say?'

'Oh, loads of jargon about Section Six of some law or other; heaven knows. It's rubbish, quite honestly; the man is barmy.'

'Crikey, Bri, what happens now?'

I felt anxious about him having to be at the house to deal with the business there, if this mad fellow was going to be there too. Brian shrugged. We stopped at the traffic lights before crossing the river over Hammersmith Bridge, and he turned to look at me and grinned.

'As Winston Churchill used to say, my love… KBO. That's what we have to do now. Keep Buggering On!'

We laughed together. It was an appropriate phrase for us in that difficult year, when weighed down with worries and stress, we had little alternative but to do exactly that.

Chapter Twelve

'I'm so tired, Bri,' I moaned, struggling out of bed as the alarm sounded loudly on the cupboard by my pillow. I hadn't been sleeping well, and as always, just as the morning arrived and the clock clicked into action to herald the day, I fell deeply asleep. 'I feel as though I've only had about an hour all night.' Yawning, I rubbed my eyes and pulled my fingers through my tousled hair.

Brian was already out of bed, pulling on his check dressing gown and heading for the kitchen to make early morning tea. He always slept well, but snored loudly and irritatingly when stressed and anxious, which served all the better to keep me awake.

'Sorry, love, was I noisy?'

He pulled the curtains and screwed up his nose at the sight of rain and wet pavements.

'It's a lousy day again. Tea won't be long.'

I flicked the television remote control and lay watching the breakfast news. It was seven a.m.

We sat in bed and drank our tea, steaming in the Jemima Puddleduck mug, and the one with the lovely Welsh terrier on it, with the chip in the handle.

'What's today for you, then?' I asked.

'I need to do a few hours at the computer first,' Brian said, 'and then I must head over to Elmwood again. There are piles of papers and legal documents that I need to collect to work on, to do with Gordon's estate. I really want to get all of that sorted out as fast as I can.'

'Well, I'm delivering a batch of flapjacks to the gym first thing,' I said, finishing my tea and making the first move out of bed. 'And then I'll come back for lunch with you here. Maybe we could go to Elmwood together after that.'

'Good idea. We need to decide what's to be done about cleaning the house, and I'll talk to Frank Willis and the girl at the RSPCA. What was her name again?'

I smiled at Brian's lack of memory on this point; he simply could not get hold of Rowena Blunt's name, the girl in the RSPCA legacy department.

'Rowena.'

'That's right. Why can't I ever remember? Daft. Well, anyway, I ought to find out what's to be done with all Gordon's things, and she's the one to tell me that.'

Gordon's will stated that his entire estate was to go to the RSPCA, and as he no longer owned a property, the entire bequest to the charity sat in his bank and building society accounts and the very large number of shares and bonds he owned. Nothing at all for his son Paul.

I went into the bathroom, leaving the door open to continue our conversation.

'You know what I've thought,' I called, 'we need to say whose things are what, because some will rightfully belong to the RSPCA, and the rest to the Cats' Charity, won't they? And what's to be done with it all, anyway?'

'So much to sort out,' Brian sighed as he selected a clean shirt from his wardrobe. 'I dare say both charities would be glad for us to go through everything, and clear the rubbish for a start. There's no one else who could say what antiques or valuables belong to whom, other than us. And then I suppose it will all go to auction, or be sold on.'

'It's wicked, really,' I said, brushing my hair. 'So much of it should be yours, and Louise's. Family things, all Aunt Helen's stuff. And Uncle Tom's,' I added indignantly. 'Let alone the money.'

'Well,' Brian sighed, 'there's no use dwelling on all of that. We'll not make it any different, and we must just accept that there's nothing for any of us; except a load of hard and dirty work,' he added.

How right he was.

I packaged my home-made flapjacks and some shortbread for sale, and drove it to Wimbledon for the coffee shop in the gym. Andrew was in his office, knee-deep in bills.

'Oh Mum, this is just hell,' he said, looking up as I leant on the side of the office door. 'The money is going out so much faster than it's coming in. I don't know what to do…'

I gave him a hug and worried with him. The future of his business looked very grave indeed.

'Thank God for Mary,' he said, looking lovingly at a snapshot of their wedding on the wall beside his desk.

'She's been so fantastic; I don't know how I'd cope without her.'

After lunch Brian and I drove to Elmwood in the rain. The house looked bleak and the side garden beside the drive was horribly overgrown with weeds.

We discovered a mess of splintered wood around the front door lock.

'God, Brian, have there been burglars again?' I exclaimed, pushing the door to see if the lock was broken. He examined it.

'No, look, the lock's been changed. I think Trevor told me after Frank's visit that he was going to. He said so many people have keys, and they can't be trusted. '

'Oh, and he can, I suppose?' I snorted. We rang the bell.

While we waited for Trevor to let us in, I read the large paper sign he had erected on the door pane.

In an almost illegible scrawl and printed in thick felt pen, was a horrendously long sentence, lacking in any form of punctuation, and meaning nothing to the reader.

I dug Brian in the ribs.

'What in heaven's name is all this about?' I asked, and he grinned.

'No idea, love. It's a load of rubbish, as far as I can see.'

'What does this 'Section Six' bit refer to? It's a threat, isn't it? To anyone who enters the house, it says… they'll be reported to the police under section six of the law.'

The door opened, and Brian and I greeted Trevor, making our way inside through the wooden planks that had been nailed to the door opening to bar the entrance.

'I've got a key for you, Brian,' Trevor said, feeling in his pocket. The trousers were the same shabby ones he always wore, but I noticed that his jumper was an old one of Gordon's, much too big for him and far from clean.

'Thanks, Trevor. How have you been?'

I realised that Brian was being diplomatic by staying in favour with Trevor, given that we would need to visit Elmwood quite frequently for the time being, and at present he seemed determined to stay in the house.

Trevor shook his head and sat down in a heap on the stairs.

'I'm not well today,' he said miserably. 'I stayed in bed till lunchtime. I'm a sick man, you know,' he added pitifully, but my suspicions were roused.

'Well, we'll not trouble you… I doubt if we'll be here long,' Brian said. 'I just need to collect some account details and so forth; we'll have a root around.'

Trevor followed us around like a shadow, watching our every move as though he owned the house and we were intruders. I checked one of the drawers in Aunt Helen's bedroom.

'Don't touch anything in there!' he shouted at me. 'I can have you in court, you know, under section six! You leave everything alone!'

'Trevor,' I said gently, more than a little ruffled. Brian was downstairs in the study. 'I'm only having a look in here to see what's to be done. None of us is entitled to remove anything valuable; we know that. Despite,' I added quietly, 'the fact that most of the treasures in this house belonged to the Fawley family once.'

Trevor's expression changed from anger to understanding.

'It's a crying shame,' he said. 'You should have all that jewellery… there's lots of expensive stuff in that top drawer.'

He had obviously had a good delve about himself, I realised, and yet he was fiercely protective of the property to the point of attempting to bar the family from doing their job. I decided not to cross this unstable man in any way if I wanted to maintain access to the house, and thereby help Brian with all he had to do.

All the drawers in Aunt Helen's room were stuffed full of her old belongings, where they had been, untouched now, for nine years. It was hard to tell whether the rotting, dank smell was emanating from the open drawers, or whether it was just the atmosphere that hung in the room in general.

It was a dark afternoon and the rain had hardly stopped all day. The light bulbs in the house had all been changed some while ago to low wattage ones so as to conserve costs, and the gloom in the bedroom was faintly eerie as the natural light outside faded. I found it hard to determine the details of the contents of the deepest drawers, and felt around cautiously for fear of disturbing nests of spiders or worse. Most of Aunt Helen's clothes had remained intact, but many items were so old that the lace and net and fine fabrics had rotted away. There were several evening bags encrusted with jewels, and many pairs of elbow-length pale leather gloves. In a higher drawer were small delicate items of underwear... Aunt Helen had been a tiny lady; and silk night-dresses and bedjackets embroidered with minute pearls.

The top two drawers were smaller though deep, sitting one beside the other in the chest. They both contained personal items like trinkets, talcum powder and make-up. Pretty lace handker-chiefs were neatly folded in a satin pouch. There was a green leather jewellery box.

I snicked open the latch to discover necklaces and bracelets of many designs, lengths and colours, but all were paste. The sparkling stones were fake gems, and the gilt of their settings tarnished. There were earrings, loads of pairs; but none I esti-mated were of any value. Just costume jewellery, like the big brooches in individual boxes in the drawer. And then I saw the row of small, square leather boxes, old and worn, but once containing rings of serious value, I felt sure. The jewellers' names on the boxes were from Hatton Garden in London, and some had crowns above the names, showing they were jewellers to royalty. I looked inside.

Without exception, the ring boxes were empty; their slots in the worn plush velvet bare, where rings had once nestled. I found long, narrow boxes too, once having contained precious necklaces and bracelets, but all had been removed.

I turned to question Trevor carefully, but he was no longer in the room, having sloped quietly away when he saw me checking the boxes. Interesting, I thought, but whatever I suspected, there could be no proof, and therefore, no accusation.

Chapter Thirteen

Four trips to Elmwood later, we had collected several carloads of paperwork and family documents, which Brian wanted to work through at home. We laid a sheet on the sitting room floor in front of the fireplace, and dusted the boxes and files before sorting them. Everything was filthy, and our hands black with dirt just from touching the old papers.

It was a Saturday evening at the very end of February, and we ate fish and chips from the local shop, looking at the stack of paperwork to be checked.

'Crikey, Mags, this will take forever,' Brian sighed. 'I hardly know where to begin. But it must be done; I can't leave anything unsorted in case it's important. We'll probably chuck just about all of this out.'

'Well there's loads more where that all came from,' I said despondently. 'I'll get some rubbish sacks.'

We finished our hasty meal and I brewed the coffee in the kitchen while I hunted out some sacks. Brian was sitting on the floor amidst the piles of papers, and we discarded most of each stack.

'Who on earth would keep every single trade receipt and bill over sixty years?' Brian said, aghast. Gordon had been a terrible hoarder, and I doubted whether he had ever looked at these slips more than once.

Here and there was a photograph; Gordon as a young man in a garden, Aunt Helen with the cats, smiling by the pond here at Elmwood. Gordon down by the river, turning cheekily to look at the camera. Gordon at his desk, writing.

I liked the photographs; each one seemed to tell a story, and I wondered what it was.

We found several beautiful photograph albums in an old case; each bound in fine black leather, with black card pages on which was tiny, neat white painted writing.

'Brian, look! These are all albums of Malcolm! As a baby… see… and then the next one as a toddler, and a little chap. Then this final one shows him as an older boy. Oh, I love these. Look, this was your cousin, Bri.'

Beautiful photos, all black and white of course, and so lovingly and carefully mounted, with descriptions and dates under each one.

'I suppose this tiny printing in the white ink is Aunt Helen's,' I said. 'Look how beautifully she's done it, what a labour of love, eh?'

Malcolm had clearly been more than a precious child to Aunt Helen, but I remembered how she and Uncle Tom had previously lost their twin baby boys. I supposed that made Malcolm all the more special when he came along.

'He looks a happy baby, doesn't he?'

'Hmm, I suppose he does. No reason not to, was there?' Brian seemed rather more interested in Gordon's old accounts.

'Well no, but I just think he looks a particularly cherished child, somehow. Lovely neat clothes, beautiful toys, this gorgeous big pram. And he's chubby and always smiling.'

In the third album, Aunt Helen featured with Malcolm in several pictures, and the captions read:

'Feeding the cats together.'

'A picnic in Richmond Park, just us two.'

'Malcolm and me, 1944, aged 8.'

A much-adored son, of that there was no doubt.

'Not many pictures of Uncle Tom,' I commented, and Brian turned from the accounts to flick through the albums.

'Probably because he was behind the camera, taking these,' he said.

'Oh look, here's one, with a train set. And another, feeding Malcolm with some baby meal or other. He doesn't look entirely comfortable with that!'

Brian laughed.

'I think Malcolm was probably a mummy's boy,' he surmised. 'And Uncle Tom would have wanted a keen young sportsman, like he'd been himself, I'd say. There aren't any pictures of Malcolm with a cricket bat, or playing football, are there?'

I had to agree.

'No, you're right. Still, I'm sure Uncle Tom really loved him. All fathers do, don't they; proper fathers?'

'Well, old Gordon didn't love poor Paul,' Brian said.

'Hmm.'

We drank our coffee in a thoughtful silence.

Two days later, Paul Lench's wife Linda telephoned. Brian answered the call in our office at home, while I was cleaning the oven after baking. He came into the kitchen to find me elbow-deep in suds and oven cleaner at the sink.

'Hold still... smudge.'

He wiped my cheek with his finger.

'That was Linda on the phone... Paul's wife.'

'What did she want?'

'Well, oddly enough, an old train set.'

'Oh...' I remembered having seen a very old and dirty Hornby box in the dining room at Elmwood amongst Gordon's old belongings that were stacked in piles on the floor.

'I've seen it. Under the front window, in the dining room.'

I squeezed out my sponge and gave a final wipe to the open oven door.

'Well, they're coming over to Elmwood tomorrow,' Brian said, putting the kettle on for coffee. 'I said we'd be there to meet them; you are free, aren't you? Nothing fixed?'

'Not tomorrow, that's fine.'

I emptied the sink and removed my apron.

'Oh Bri, I wonder what they are like? I'll be interested to meet Paul.'

'Hmm. Funny that he never speaks on the phone, only Linda.'

I decided on instant coffee for speed, and spooned it into two mugs as the kettle boiled.

'Well, from what we've heard, he seems quite shy. Although he sounded pleasant and easy-going that time he spoke to me briefly. Otherwise it's always Linda, isn't it, on the phone?'

We took our coffee to the table and sat with the biscuit tin between us.

'I said we'd be at the house about two o'clock,' Brian said. 'They have to drive over in the morning, but they're only a couple of hours from Elmwood, apparently. I said Trevor would let them in if they arrive before us, so I'll give him a ring to let him know.'

I was intrigued to meet Paul; the son around whom I had built a mystery in my mind. He was no disappointment the following day.

We arrived at Elmwood promptly at two o'clock to find Paul and Linda already at the house, an old Ford car parked in the drive to herald their presence. As we entered the hall, they were in deep and friendly conversation with Trevor who was seated on the stairs, wearing his usual grubby trousers and an old, worn sweatshirt of dubious origin. He was sipping something medicinal from a steaming mug decorated with a large marmalade cat.

Brian extended a hand to Paul, whose appearance instantly shocked me. He was an identical, but younger version of Gordon, though with a warmer smile.

'Paul, good to meet you. And you too, Linda.'

We all shook hands. Linda was a homely woman with a friendly smile and a shock of newly permed grey hair. She held two large laundry bags, and explained that they had come to take any of Gordon's things that they would like as they were rightfully Paul's.

'And my train set,' he added.

'Let me show you where…' I began, but Trevor chipped in.

'I've told them, Maggie,' he said. 'It's all ready by the window in there.'

And he nodded at the dining room door.

'While we're here we'll finish sorting those study shelves,' Brian said. 'Give us a shout if we can help.'

I, however, followed Linda to the breakfast room, where she was filling one of her bags with various silver items and some china, quite unabashed.

'I know what's what, Maggie,' she said. 'Paul and I stayed with the old man you know, all those years back when we last saw him. He'd been ill, and he contacted Paul for help, but we weren't with him long. He was next door then, of course, but he was so rude and abusive to me especially, so we packed our bags and went home. I vowed then that I'd never come here again, and that was about twenty years ago.'

I laughed politely.

'Don't tell me… I can just imagine the sort of behaviour. He was well known for his loathing of women,' I said knowingly.

'Hmph! Wasn't he just? Do this, do that; get me this, fetch me that… just as if we were servants!'

She opened a canteen of cutlery, closed the lid again, and laid it carefully in the laundry bag.

'This was his. Most of the old man's stuff… the good things… came from Paul's mother you know; her old family things.'

Linda pulled a face.

'He had nothing of course from the Lench family. Poor as church mice, they were.'

A silver teapot on a stand went into the bag. I perched on the corner of the big wooden table rather than sit on the stained old chairs, habitually used by the cats, and covered with moulted fur. Linda investigated the contents of the china cabinet, and I wondered whether she could be sure if the things she was taking were Gordon's not Aunt Helen's. However, I felt it was only right that Paul should have his mother's belongings, if indeed these were from her family home at one time, given that everything else was to go to the RSPCA.

'I'm so sorry about the will, Linda,' I said, and she shrugged, wiping her now dirty hands on an old tea towel.

'It's no surprise to us,' she said. 'Never a birthday present, never a card, not since Paul was seventeen. Didn't want him, you see, once his mother died.'

'Poor Paul, that's so dreadful.'

'Well, worse than didn't want him really, more like abused him, I'd say. Emotionally and verbally, anyway, and a fair bit of hitting him about as well.'

'Oh Linda, how awful!'

'That's when he left home, and decided to fend for himself. No help from the old man; Paul made his own way in the world. But he loved his mother,' she added, with a smile. 'Now she was a good lady, by all accounts. Came to a tragic end, though, poor soul.'

My curiosity was aroused.

'Had Paul been a happy child before she died, do you know?' I asked.

Linda nodded, and closed the cupboard door, having completed her search.

'Oh yes, I think so,' she said. 'His memories of those early days are all good ones.'

'There are photos for you to take; I've put them on one side. And a little biscuit tin that was Gordon's, with family documents, including the various certificates; you know, marriage, death, that sort of thing. Paul might like to have them... things of his mother's, so to speak.'

'No, er, ... rings, are there? Or nice jewellery?'

I smirked to myself.

'Nothing, Linda. Anything of any value in that line seems to have gone, including Aunt Helen's lovely things. I'm sure there would have been some valuable pieces at one time, but we haven't found anything.'

Linda indicated with a twitch of her head towards upstairs, and presumably Trevor.

'Do you think...?' she said, and I shrugged.

'Who knows? We can't prove a thing. He's been here since last November, when Gordon was virtually bedridden, so he's had plenty of opportunity.' I stood up. 'Anyway, Linda, it doesn't matter now. Everything left here is legally the property of the Cats' Charity or the RSPCA now. Not a single thing for any of us. Now that was Gordon's doing!'

'It's wicked, Maggie, that's what I say, just wicked! I remember all that business in the paper years ago, when Brian's aunt died. We read that, we did, and Paul said it was a crying shame. Never did go through though, did it, past the planners, I mean, for a cat shelter here?'

I shook my head.

'No, there was a local petition against it. I think the charity will just sell the house and land, now that Gordon's gone.'

Paul came into the breakfast room, dusting off his hands.

'Looks like you've found a fair bit, love,' he said to Linda, indicating the laundry bag and its contents.

'I've put my train set in the car, and a few more things of the old man's.'

'I'll take this out then,' Linda said, hurrying off with her spoils, as though anxious to leave as soon as she could.

Paul sat heavily on one of the undesirable chairs, and looked at me. Even the way in which he sat was reminiscent of his father, and he too, was a tall man, with Gordon's imposing build.

'My God, Paul,' I said, catching my breath. 'It's quite creepy; you're so much like your father!'

Clearly angered, his reply was a retort.

'Well, I don't see how!' he snapped. 'In fact, you see, my father wasn't my father, and my real mother was my aunt.'

'Pardon?'

I was stunned.

Paul softened and smiled, exposing irregular, poor teeth. He adjusted his glasses and explained.

'Typical of the old man, you know,' he said. 'I never knew I was adopted until I met a girl I wanted to marry, and brought her here to the old house next door to meet him. Big mistake that was; she said, just like you, that I was the spitting image of the old boy. He was furious, and told her outright that it wasn't possible, because he and my mother had adopted me as a baby.'

'But what did you tell me just now about your aunt?' I asked, fascinated.

I remembered having found a death certificate in the old biscuit tin for a Miss Annie Lench, Gordon's sister, who died young of breast cancer, never having married.

'She was my real mother,' Paul went on. 'Got into trouble, see when she was young, and the old devil did what he could by adopting me for her. No one knew who my father was.'

'That was good of Gordon's wife… your mother,' I said, and Paul nodded, smiling.

'Ah, yes, now she was a lovely woman, my mother,' he said. 'A really good woman, and always good to me. Not like him,' he spat.

No love lost between them, it was clear.

At that point Brian joined us, with yet more documents to remove from the house and check at home, in a box stained with damp and age. Paul was in full flow, reminiscing, and Brian leant on the doorframe to listen in.

'When my mother died,' Paul went on, 'I think he blamed me, somehow. Seemed like it, anyway, the way he treated me. Never wanted to know me after that, and I was only sixteen. Your Uncle Tom, Brian, now he was a good man, always kind to me. The only one who was, really,' he said pitifully. 'Can't say the same for her, though,' meaning Aunt Helen, surprisingly. 'She used to be cold and hard, and just told me to pull myself together and get on with life.'

'That sounds rather cruel… not like Aunt Helen at all,' Brian said, and Paul shrugged.

'Maybe not, with other people,' he continued, 'but with me she was sharp. I thought it was unkind, seeing as she had a son my age, whom she adored. Maybe she got hard after he died, you know; maybe I'm forgetting.'

Paul seemed embarrassed to have spoken badly of Brian's aunt, but I felt it had come from the heart.

'Was it around that time that Malcolm died too?' I asked.

'No, it was about three years later, and I'd gone away. We did National Service then, you see, and Malcolm died in Reading, where he was stationed, at the end of his first year. Terrible to-do that was. Terrible.'

Brian looked a little uncomfortable, and probably sensing this, Paul stopped his tale. He stood up.

'Well, better be off. I don't want to be driving back in the traffic later on. Not happy driving, really.'

Linda had returned.

'Well, I'll drive then,' she said firmly, and I suspected that she wore the trousers, so to speak.

'Come on, nothing more to do here, so best be off.'

We said our farewells and they drove away up the drive for the last time, as it happened. We didn't see Paul or Linda Lench again, but he had left me with lasting questions in my mind and an even deeper mystery surrounding Gordon to be solved.

Frank Willis telephoned when Brian was mowing the lawn; the first time for the season. It was probably too damp, and he cursed quietly as he tried against the odds to make the mower work. The pattern of up and down stripes in the grass was proving to be somewhat irregular.

'Darling! Phone! It's Frank,' I called through the sitting room window.

'Damn thing! OK, I'm coming in.'

He turned off the mower and came in through the French windows, leaving bits of damp grass across the carpet from his garden shoes. He picked up the receiver.

'Frank. Hallo, what can I do for you?' undoing his laces and removing the offending articles in the hall.

'Right. Yes, righto. Good Lord, has he really? Well, blow me down. No, I'd never have thought... well, as I say, good Lord!'

I left my ironing in the kitchen and came to listen in the hall, but Brian waved me away. He never liked me to stand near during a conversation. When he put down the receiver he came to tell me the news, looking sheepish. He put his arms around my waist from behind, and bent his chin onto my shoulder.

'Sorry, darling. Sorry. I just hate it when you listen in...'

I smiled.

'I know, you daft thing. Sorry too.'

'You'll never believe what's happened now.'

I turned to face him eagerly.

'What?'

'Trevor has officially refused to leave Elmwood. He says he now has squatters' rights, and he's turning the house into a cats' sanctuary, in accordance with Aunt Helen's wishes, he says. He said all sorts of balderdash to Frank on the phone, and the result is that he's going to be served with an eviction order next week, if he hasn't gone by Friday!'

Sharp intake of breath by us both.

'Life is nothing short of interesting, anyway,' Brian said. 'Given all the gym problems facing us all, it's light relief, I suppose.'

We laughed. In truth, light relief it was not, as it made life much more difficult for us at Elmwood.

Brian and I were making regular trips now to the house, sorting room by room, in our attempts to uncover all the essential documents Brian needed as the only executor of Gordon's will, and to help in the eventual clearing of the house. When this had been completed, the antiques were to be removed to auction, and the Cats' Charity was to arrange for all remaining less valuable items to go to their charity shops for sale. Frank had agreed that valueless family items such as the photograph albums, could be retained by us as memorabilia.

It would have been far simpler for us if every visit hadn't been hampered by Trevor, who breathed down our necks whenever we were there. He now began to assume ownership of Elmwood, and started to tell us what to do or not, as the case might be, while we were there. In view of the news of the coming eviction, Brian decided to visit Trevor the following day.

When he arrived, a large piece of sheeting, torn into a rectangle, had been draped across the window to the left of the front door, like a flag. On it was painted, in rough red lettering:

'BARNES CAT SANCTUARY. KEEP OUT!'

Inside, there were more shocks in store. Much of the upstairs study, which had been Malcolm's bedroom, had been roughly painted bright purple, and derogatory comments plastered over the plain wall about the Cats' Charity. Trevor had found photos of several much-loved cats from the past... Susie, I recognised... and had stuck them up with provocative statements beside them on the walls:

'CASH protection, NOT CATS' Protection!'

'HANDS OFF OUR HOME!'

'UNLESS YOU ARE A FELINE, ENTER IN FEAR!'

Brian was saddened to see his uncle's once-beautiful home so destroyed, and such appalling graffiti emblazoned on once-lovely walls. A skull and crossbones on a large, ragged piece of cardboard, was hanging above the desk, where Trevor had set up his own computer. A printed letter beside it stated that he had taken over the telephone bill, and paid a recent credit, thus assuming tenancy rights at the house, or so he thought.

'Look here, Trevor,' Brian said gently, sitting with him in the upstairs kitchen over a mug of coffee.

'I understand that the cats' people have told you you'll be evicted if you don't leave of your own accord by Friday. Frank Whatshisname was on the phone to me yesterday. You do understand, don't you, what they're going to do?'

Trevor looked up knowingly from his mug and grinned.

'Not only do I understand, Brian, but it's happened to me before,' he said. 'I know what I'm doing, believe me. I've told that Frank bugger I'll not go without a fight. I've got friends, you know, all ready to move in here with me, to put up resistance.'

'But why, Trevor? You know you'll be removed... forcibly if it has to come to that... and what reason do you have to stay here anyway? Is it for a roof over your head?'

'Pah! And live in this state? You must be joking!'

'Well, quite; that's why I don't understand—'

'Brian,' Trevor interrupted, banging his mug on the table, 'I've told you before, and I've told the charity people, I'm here for the sake of the cats. It's what I promised old Gordon.'

'Oh, come on, Trevor, pull the other one. We both know Gordon never intended you to stay on here forever; he told me himself that Coco was to be re-homed in the event of his death. I'd asked ages ago what he wanted with regard to old Coco...'

'Ah! But what about the others?'

Trevor's voice was raised.

'What others? The outside strays, do you mean?'

Trevor started to count on his fingers, and mentioned the names of several cats long dead, and buried in the garden under named tombstones.

'Old Smokey's out there now,' he said, standing up and looking through the filthy windowpane.

Brian could see a fat, elderly black cat with a white bib, slowly meandering its way from the shelter across the overgrown garden. Nearby was a prettier, tortoiseshell creature, and Trevor looked at his watch.

'Time for their dinner. They know, you know! I'll have to go down.'

Brian watched, fascinated, as Trevor opened tins of cat food by the sink, and shared it into bowls. Coco had arrived in the kitchen and was mewing as she rubbed against his legs, sensing mealtime.

'There you are, my lovely, who's a good girl, then?'

A large tin of pilchards was then opened, and several of the fish placed neatly on the tops of the dishes for the garden cats. Coco was not so lucky.

'Why the special extras?' Brian asked, and Trevor gave a knowing, secret smile.

'Just for the strays,' he said, making his way downstairs with the bowls. 'Keeps them coming, see? Wouldn't want to lose them now, would I?'

Amazingly, Trevor kept us amicably in the picture. The day of his eviction case at court arrived, and he telephoned Brian in the morning, to tell him what was going on.

Brian was working in his study at home, and when he finished the call, he hurried in to the kitchen where I was baking.

'Mags, you'll never believe it!'

'What?'

'Trevor on the phone; he's off to court at 2 p.m. today but this morning he's organised for the press to be at the house to interview him, and to cover his case at court. He says he'll be on the local news on TV tonight, and he's going to give Frank Willis and the Cats' Charity a good dressing down! Should be in the papers tomorrow, he says.'

'Good Lord!' I sifted flour into my bowl so vigorously that clouds of it filled the air and settled on the worktop like a thin veil.

'There's no end to all this, it seems,' Brian sighed. 'And I've had a call from Andrew too; the gym is going up for sale. What a year we're having, my old love, eh?'

He put the kettle on to boil for tea, and we shared the sad moment. Uncle Tom's beautiful old house vandalised, and after so much hard work and struggling, Andrew's business going under. It was indeed, a difficult year for us.

That evening, I served our shepherd's pie on trays, to eat while we watched the local news on television, and sure enough, there was Elmwood on the screen, and Trevor Hill on a garden chair, with a cat on his lap.

The phone rang... it was Louise.

'Maggie; are you watching BBC? It's that man... Trevor 'thing'... but he's so clean!'

'Yes, we're looking now! Thanks; I'll ring you back.'

Louise was right, Trevor did indeed look clean. He was clean-shaven and his hair neat, and he wore a smart tweed jacket and a cap, which gave him the air of a country gent. The television coverage then switched to outside the courtroom, and he was interviewed again; on both occasions slating the Cats' Charity and suggesting in no uncertain terms that they were taking money under false pretences, and that the welfare of cats was of no importance to them at all.

The following morning in all the national newspapers there were photographs and reports about Trevor and the case, mentioning Sir Tom and Lady Fawley and the original bequest to the charity.

Trevor, however, benefited little. He was served with a legal eviction order, giving him two more weeks in which to gather his possessions together and leave Elmwood.

All, however, was not yet over.

Chapter Fourteen

I sat in the hairdresser's having my highlights done, on a Thursday morning at the beginning of March.

'So he's to go on the fourth,' I told Maria, who faithfully altered my naturally greying hair colour to a warm honey brown with blonde streaks every four months or so, and caught up on the recent gossip as she did so.

Maria folded foil squares onto my hair, her beautiful dark Cypriot eyes wide.

'Would you ever believe it?' she said. 'Such a story, Maggie, you should write it all down. So much money, and all your family treasures. I cannot believe there's nothing for any of you... all for the cats!'

'And the RSPCA, now,' I added, 'since old Gordon died. Oh well, that's just the way life goes, I suppose. Nothing to be done.'

She finished spiking me with foil and pulled off her bleaching gloves.

'There now, you're finished for the next little while. Sit and relax; I'll get you a coffee.'

'Thanks, Maria, you're a star. I really need this today, apart from my hair. I just need some time out, away from all the worries.'

'Your Andrew, is it? And his gym?'

'Mmm... things are really bad there, I'm afraid. It's up for sale, but no one's interested so far. The money's all gone, and Brian and I are paying the wages, just to keep it going for a takeover to happen. Our money's disappearing so fast...'

'You said that a few months ago...'

Maria pulled up her swivelling stool and sat down. The shop was unusually quiet today.

'Yes, I did... and now we're really desperate. It's just going like sand through our fingers, Maria; I'm so afraid for us all quite honestly.'

She put a comforting hand on my shoulder.

'You'll be all right, Maggie, you'll see. It will all come right in the end, don't you worry. I've had my bad times too, but things are going well again now. Just keep cheerful… you always are.'

I smiled. Maria was so encouraging, with just the right amount of sympathetic understanding thrown in.

The shop phone rang… another client to book an appointment, and she went to take the call.

'Yes, right… let me look in the book.'

I sat peacefully in my tin foil headgear, and read a magazine about film stars and their luxurious Hollywood residences. A far cry from our own situation, I thought, since our house, home to the family for almost thirty years, was also up for sale. Sadly, Brian and I were forced to sell to clear our debts, incurred when we took out a massive new mortgage to help Andrew with the gym. It was hard work keeping the house pristine for viewers, and they seemed to be few and far between.

We visited Elmwood the day before Trevor had to leave, and saw to our surprise a large green van parked in the drive. It had windows in the driver's cab at the front, but the back section, large enough for minor house removals, was totally enclosed.

'Whose is this?' I said, as we parked the car behind it and went to peer inside.

'Can't see anything,' Brian said, taller than I, and therefore able to look through the cab window.

'It's just two seats up here and the back container section is sealed off.'

'But whose is it?'

He pulled a silly face.

'Now how would I know, you daft woman? Come on, we'll find Trevor.'

We let ourselves in through the makeshift barricade in the doorway, and called upstairs to tell Trevor we had arrived.

He came slowly downstairs, looking his slovenly self once more after his total change of appearance for the press and court interviews. Even the scruffy beard was beginning to grow again.

'Hi, Trevor. There's a green van in the drive.'

Trevor nodded.

'It's mine,' he said, surprisingly.

'Oh! I thought you had a car... the day of the funeral...' I said.

'I have. And the van, too.' Trevor smiled slyly, and I wondered, without asking, where he normally parked these two vehicles, which had never been seen nearby since he took up residence the previous November. I also wondered very seriously what was in the back of the van; closed to view and large enough to accommodate a fair bit of antique furniture and other things besides.

The doors to all the downstairs rooms at Elmwood were always kept closed, and Trevor appeared to be living, as Gordon had, on the upper two floors, with Coco the cat for company. There was no sign of the afore-mentioned 'friends' whom he had expected to move in and cause resistance.

He was a strange and surprising man; usually friendly towards Brian and myself, but certainly aggressive in his comments about any form of authority. He seemed to spend his life going from place to place causing trouble, and proudly told us how he often went on marches, or staged sit-ins that were fundamentally anti-establishment.

Brian and I chose not to question Trevor too fully about the reason for, or indeed the contents of the van, but then he told us that he had emptied all the old clothes into sacks and was taking them to another animal charity somewhere in Surrey.

'Don't know if I believe him, unless there's money in it for him,' Brian said in an undertone, when Trevor went out to his van. I watched through the doorway; he locked the cab and returned at once, thereby ensuring that any contents would remain safe and unseen.

'Poor old Coco,' Trevor said, petting her on his return. 'That Frank fellow told me on the phone that she's to be collected and re-homed tomorrow. Sad day, that'll be.'

'What about the strays, then, Trevor?' I asked.

'They're going too. Heartless, that charity, I tell you. They'll probably put them all down.'

Interestingly, Frank Willis had spoken to Brian on the phone after unearthing quite a scandal surrounding the strays. Someone from the charity had visited Elmwood to ascertain the number of cats for re-homing, and met a local resident on her way in. This lady told her about the time just before the eviction case in court, when she too had called at the house for a certain reason, and had followed Trevor inside. Apparently she tried to enter the breakfast room at the back and was rebuffed severely by Trevor, who was keeping at least ten cats shut up in there, and who was very anxious in case any got out.

The lady from the charity then called on all the houses in Gumber Lane, to ascertain whether anyone's wandering cat fitted the description of the garden moggies, and two, it seemed, most certainly did. The third, old black Smokey, as Trevor called him, in fact belonged to an elderly lady quite a distance away, and it was thought that Trevor had kidnapped him (probably in the van) and driven him the distance so that he couldn't return home. Brian remembered the pilchards on the strays' dinners, and realised that they were being lured into the garden and tempted, with tasty food, to remain. This, thought the foolish man, gave him reason to remain in the house, as he was sole carer for all these resident felines.

'Smokey' had been tagged with an electronic 'chip' which effectively proved the elderly lady's ownership. She was more than delighted to have him back. The remaining local cats soon returned home over the course of the next weeks, once the tit-bits and tasty meals were no longer provided.

The cat problem solved, I was still concerned about Trevor, and the opportunities he had had to help himself to Elmwood's contents.

'Bri, what should we do?' I asked. 'What if he's making off with valuable stuff in that van?'

Brian wasn't unduly worried.

'Not much we can do, as far as I can see,' he said. 'And anyway, if he has got the odd treasure or two, there's still a fortune here for the two charities. I think we ask no further; what the eye doesn't see... But maybe I'll just advise Frank about it on the phone.'

I nodded in agreement. Surely, given the lifestyle he chose to live, Trevor Hill could do with a few comforts as much as the animals the charities would support with the money they were to receive.

We unlocked the two large living room doors and checked, as far as we were able in the half light, that essential antiques had not been removed. A complete mess met our eyes; drawers had been disturbed in the sideboards, and cupboard doors were open though contents remained inside. Boxes belonging to Gordon were open, and contents in disarray around the floor and on the table. It was impossible to tell if anything was missing.

Trevor stood behind us in the doorway of the dining room, his hands in his pockets.

I picked up a lovely old inlaid wooden box that I hadn't seen before.

'What's this?'

'Used to be war medals in there,' Trevor volunteered.

I opened the lid and saw that it was empty; the velvet lining with markers and sections for eight medals completely bare.

'Well, where are they, then?' I asked, looking directly at Trevor. He smiled his sly smile, one corner of his mouth turning slowly up.

'I don't know,' he said.

Neither of us believed him for a moment, but we were wiser than to say so.

During our conversation with Trevor that day, I mentioned an Oscar Wilde play that our amateur dramatic group was to stage in the summer. The wardrobe mistress had put out a plea for suitable dresses for the ladies in the cast, and I decided to test Trevor's story about old clothes going to a charity.

'Trevor, in your sorting out, did you find any of Aunt Helen's old evening dresses?' I asked. 'Short or long ones would do; our drama group at church needs some for their next production.'

Very willingly, Trevor offered to find some dresses for me, and disappeared to his van, while Brian and I continued our turning out operation in the study downstairs. After what seemed like quite a while, he returned with a midnight blue lace dress and jacket over his arm, and a long black satin evening dress held high, so that the hem stayed clean.

'These do?'

'Oh Trevor, thank you. I remember that blue lace one... they're so tiny, aren't they? Look at the nipped in waists; I think they'll be too small for the ladies in our play, actually, but I'll take them to see.'

He laid them both over the back of the study armchair.

'I'll be off then,' he said, jiggling keys in his pocket. 'And I'm sleeping here tonight before leaving for good tomorrow.'

He turned to Brian.

'I'm not going to contest it after all, Brian. May as well leave peacefully, when all the cats are gone. Poor little Coco,' he added with feeling.

'Well, a wise decision, I'm sure Trevor,' Brian said. 'We'll not see you again then, after today.'

He offered his hand, and Trevor shook it with a smile.

'I'll leave my keys,' he said. 'That Frank fellow said to deliver them to the agent along at the shops. I'll be off to another project then, tomorrow.'

He went up the stairs and disappeared into the bedroom on the top floor that had been his home, dirt and all, for the last four months. When he was out of earshot, I looked enquiringly at Brian.

'Another project, did he say?'

'Hmm, I noticed that too.'

'What does he mean, do you think?'

'Oh, I imagine he'll find another elderly soul with a hefty bank balance somewhere and move in there for a while. Perhaps it's his line of business, Mags. I expect he's managed to 'milk' a few old souls to his advantage before now, but I fear he was somewhat unlucky where our Gordon was concerned.'

I pulled a face.

'Don't, Bri! He wasn't *our* Gordon!'

Brian laughed.

'Indeed not; just a figure of speech, love. Now, let's go through these boxes and clear the junk. I'm filthy already, look.'

He showed me his hands, and then wiped them on his trousers; grubby gardening ones, worn for the occasion and the task. We began turning out the stack of boxes, obviously untouched for heaven knows how many years. Clouds of dust flew up as I snapped the string, and I coughed as I lifted the lid.

'Oh, Bri... letters. Loads of them, all in piles. Look at this.'

I sat on my heels on the dirty, worn carpet, and read one pile of envelopes… small ones; some coloured, mostly yellowing white, some brown. Almost all were handwritten, and addressed: 'Mr & Mrs Thomas Fawley.', 'Mr Tom Fawley', 'Mrs T. Fawley', or 'Mr & Mrs T. Fawley'.

All letters therefore, sent in the early years, before Uncle Tom's knighthood, after which envelopes were all addressed to 'Sir Thomas and Lady Fawley'.

I looked at the date stamp and all the letters were sent in November or December, 1955. The date made me gasp, as something registered in my memory.

'Oh Brian… look at these! They are all sympathy letters I think; sent after Malcolm died…'

Brian squatted beside me and took a thin sheet of aged white paper to read.

One letter after another; so many letters. So many friends, work colleagues, business and scientific associates. Neighbours, Sea Scouts, groups of all sorts to whom Uncle Tom was affiliated or belonged, at so many different levels. And all of them so sorry to hear the news, saddened to learn of their loss, their grief; the devastation that was the death of an only son.

I wiped my eyes with a dusty finger, leaving a grey streak down each cheek.

'So sad,' I said quietly.

Brian nodded in agreement, and with emotion in his voice, said:

'Poor Uncle Tom. Poor Aunt Helen. How terrible it must have been for them.'

'Just imagine, Bri, all these letters tumbling through that letterbox in the hallway; all these! Would it help, do you think, if you were grieving, to have to read all these?'

'And answer them.' He pointed to Aunt Helen's tiny writing in the corners of each envelope, stating 'answered', with the appropriate date.

'Yes, Aunt Helen would certainly have done that,' I said, remembering how we always received her little 'thank you' notes after every family tea, or lunch, or special celebration party. Also after every present received from us; the children's simple gifts at

134

Christmas, and the little holiday souvenirs (usually of a feline theme) so personally chosen. Aunt Helen had always been appreciative.

We read a number of letters and replaced them in their box, putting it carefully to one side to take home. I wanted to read every one, and the afternoon was drawing to a close.

'You look tired, darling.' Brian put his hand on my shoulder. 'Let's call it a day. We've cleared loads; look at all this, for the rubbish pile...'

Certainly we had worked hard, filling six large rubbish sacks with old paper, magazines and junk from the shelves and desk drawers in the study. The boxes of letters and personal papers had been tied with string so many years ago, and I suspected, never looked at since. What, I wondered, was in the others in that pile? What had we discovered, and what, indeed, might we yet discover in the unopened boxes? We carried then carefully, three in all, to our car, blowing and dusting the dirt off as best we could.

In one corner of the study lay the three tan leather attaché cases. My interest was roused. What would we find in these, I wondered, bearing in mind the harrowing contents of box number one. The cases looked personal, as opposed to the business-like document files that we had just sorted and mainly discarded into rubbish sacks. Most of those contained old receipts and insurance papers.

I indicated the tan cases. 'What about these, Bri? Shall we take them home too? Time is getting on, and we need to feed the dogs.'

'Righto, as you wish. I expect there's nothing much in them, but we'll have a look later. Here, let me take them... are they heavy?'

Brian picked up two of the three small cases and they promptly snapped off at the handles, brittle and weak with age. One case opened as it hit the floor, and spilt its contents onto the carpet at our feet.

'More letters! My God, what are these, then?'

Brian picked up an old brown envelope, with a formal, typed address. I was busy pushing the stray contents back into the case, wanting to get home.

'This one's from the MOD,' he read. 'Something to do with the army…'

'Come on, Bri, let's go. We'll look at it all at home.'

I looked up to see Brian's expression change as he read the letter, and he sat down heavily on the old leather chair by the desk.

'It's about Malcolm, Mags,' he said in a subdued voice. 'About why he died…'

I put my arm around his shoulders and adjusted my glasses again to read the tiny print of the letter, but as I began, Trevor appeared in the study doorway.

'You two still here?' he said.

'We're just going. Got a bit carried away with the clearing out.'

Brian stood up, thrusting the letter in his hand back into its case and closing the lid.

We drove home quietly, both of us deep in thought; reflecting on the sadness of a couple who had lost so much amidst wealth and beauty which meant so little to them in comparison.

'No wonder they were strange, Bri,' I mused. 'Especially Aunt Helen. What it must have done to her, losing Malcolm like that, on the edge of manhood. I'm so, so sorry for them both.'

The tan cases and the cardboard boxes sat wedged together in the back of the car. I wondered apprehensively what else we would discover when we searched through the rest of their contents, and a cool finger of unease touched me swiftly.

What secrets did Elmwood hold? What were we to discover, amidst the squalor that was left?

Chapter Fifteen

Another visit, and a small red van was parked in the drive this time, instead of Trevor's large green one. This van had 'The Cats' Charity' emblazoned on one side, and a row of cartoon character cats beneath it, all smiling.

We let ourselves in through the open door and found a small, spiky little lady inside, wearing an orange fluffy jumper which reminded me of marmalade fur.

'She's even got the whiskers!' Brian whispered as she scurried through to the breakfast room carrying a white plastic cat carrier.

'I suppose she's after Coco,' I said, feeling sorry for the poor old thing, whose life had been turned upside down after Gordon left. The lady returned, speaking calmly to the occupant of the box in her hands, and as she approached I noticed that she did indeed have a fairly prolific growth of facial hair above her top lip, as Brian had mentioned.

We introduced ourselves and the top lip smiled, exposing some pretty scary teeth.

'May Groombridge,' she said. 'I'm here to collect this little poppet.'

Her voice rose to a squeak as she peered through the carrier slats.

'Aren't I, my beauty? Little Coco, I believe, for re-homing.'

Coco mewed piteously, and I felt truly sad to see her go. She had welcomed us with a rub around our legs on every occasion that we had visited, and this was, after all, her home. Now she sat trapped in a white plastic box, to be taken to a new place with new people. I wanted to give her a stroke, but the box was clipped tight.

'Oh no, dear,' said May firmly, at my request. 'She'd be off and away quick as a flash, and it's taken me quite a while to get her in here, I can tell you. Had to resort to a sardine in the end.'

There was a tell-tale aroma in the region of May, and I was

glad if Coco had enjoyed the lure. We watched the red van leave with her inside and May driving at speed straight into the lane.

'Phew!' said Brian with a grin. 'Could have been a near miss if anyone had been driving past. She was a character all right.'

'The Cats' people must have a key,' I pondered, 'as Trevor has now gone. I suppose they will be in and out to collect things for the charity shops, as Frank told you on the phone.'

Sure enough, two pleasant ladies called Beryl and Sally arrived during the afternoon in a black estate car, and came hurrying in before we left.

'Hallo, I'm Beryl,' the taller of the two told us with a smile. She wore leopard-skin print leggings and a black jumper, on which I detected quite a bit of cat fur. Sally, her colleague, was round and jolly, and smelt of smoke. Almost as soon as we were done with the introductions she went outside to the car.

'Just a five-minute fag break,' she said, leaving Beryl with a roll of plastic sacks for treasures she thought would be saleable in a charity shop.

Brian and I began the clearout upstairs. I ventured into the top floor bedroom where Trevor had slept, and found an old mattress on the floor, and very little else. He had taken his rubbish, surprisingly, and though the room was dirty, it wasn't untidy. The air however smelt stale, and I opened the window to freshen it. The wooden surround was rotten and crumbling, and I wondered whether it had been opened at all for years.

'I'll do Aunt Helen's room, while you're in here,' I suggested to Brian, who was already clearing Malcolm's old bedroom, now Gordon's old study. He had brought his own old desk in here from next door, and a filing cabinet, full, it seemed, of engineering books and knick-knacks. Various little gadgets were contained in the deep metal drawers; pipe cleaners and cigar cutters, (the drawer which held these reeked of stale tobacco) several electrical oddments and reels of wire, and hundreds upon hundreds of receipts, bills and bits of paper of no consequence at all.

'God, Mags, look at all this! I've got to go through the lot, but I'm sure it's all complete rubbish. It'll take hours. I'm tempted to bin the entire lot, but if I do, there'll be something important lost. Oh well, here goes.'

Poor Brian; so much work and involvement. I looked at him anxiously, noting his bothered frown and the weary slump of his shoulders as he set to work in the filing cabinet drawers.

I could hear Beryl and Sally moving china and glass from cupboards downstairs, and calling to each other as they went from room to room. We all worked busily for some while, and then I went to the upstairs kitchen to make tea. I had brought our own kettle, mugs and provisions as I didn't trust anything in the house to be clean.

'Beryl! Sally!' I leant over the banisters and saw Sally below with a crate load of crockery and vases, on her way to the van.

'I'm making tea up here... can I do some for you two?'

'Mmm, lovely, thanks. Both white, no sugar.'

I scoured out an extra two mugs and brewed tea for us all, taking the two ladies' downstairs first. They sat on the stairs to drink it, the leopard-skin leggings two steps higher than Sally in her voluminous beige jumper with roses on the front.

'Thanks, Maggie, we needed this.' Beryl smiled. Both ladies were so friendly. We joined them for our tea.

'Has anyone mentioned the auctioneer's visit to you?' Sally asked. 'I gather from Frank Willis that a chap is coming tomorrow to value antiques. We're just taking everything else that might be saleable, you understand.'

Brian nodded, confirming that he knew about the auctioneer's visit, and agreeing to be at the house to let him in, now that Trevor had gone.

'Before you arrived we found some old family things in the loft,' Beryl said. 'I dare say you'd like to take those. There's a pile of old books with inscriptions in, not modern enough for our shop, and you might like to keep some of them. I'll bring everything onto the landing for you, to see if you want it.'

'I know what I would really like,' Brian said, 'and that's our old family clock from the dining room. And the other one that was meant for my sister, from the drawing room.'

He proceeded to tell the story of the will, and the notes written by Aunt Helen and found in the pendulum cases after her death. While he talked, I returned to the bedroom to sort the drawers of Aunt Helen's personal belongings.

To our surprise, the front door in the hallway opened, and Trevor Hill came in.

'Trevor! We thought you'd left,' Brian said.

He smiled his sly grin.

'Yes… well, I'm only back for a couple of days. My new place isn't ready yet.'

He was clearly disturbed to find us all at the house, and I noticed he carried a full rucksack as he disappeared back to his old and empty room upstairs.

I raised my eyebrows as I looked at Brian, having come out of the bedroom when I heard Trevor's voice.

'What's he doing back?' I whispered, and Brian shrugged.

'No idea; he says his new place isn't ready for a couple of days. I'll phone Frank to let him know when we get home. Trevor can't keep coming and going like this; he obviously hasn't returned his key as he said he would.'

'Unless he'd had another one cut,' I thought suspiciously. What was the man up to?

We worked for a further hour before going home, and saw Beryl and Sally off in the red van together with a fair collection of trinkets and crockery, flower vases and small items for the shop. Everything was grubby, and I hoped that they would give it all a good clean up before attempting to sell anything to the public. Trevor's door on the top floor was firmly closed, and he didn't reappear before we left.

'I've collected all these bits and pieces to sort at home,' I told Brian, putting several shopping bags of personal items into the car. He, also, had paperwork to check, and both of us were filthy.

'I've washed my hands twice,' I said, 'but I still feel grubby.'

Brian agreed.

'And now I'm back here again tomorrow!' he moaned. 'The hours I'm putting in, Mags, and all for absolutely nothing!'

'The charity shop is doing quite nicely,' I commented. 'Beryl says they always make lots of money on the ordinary stuff, let alone the antiques at auction. It all seems so unfair…'

'Well, it won't do us any good to dwell on it, love. Nothing to be done; best accept it, that's what I think.'

We drove slowly home through the rush hour traffic at the end of the day, feeling used and abused and very much let down. All around us at Elmwood were family belongings which should rightfully now be Brian's and Louise's, but instead it was all going to benefit cats, and from the things that were Gordon's, the RSPCA. It came at a time when we were financially desperate ourselves, and to cap it all, Brian was working so hard for the two charities; clearing, sorting and dealing with horrendous mess and squalor, and giving hours of his time being available when needed at the house.

'If this is justice, I'm a one-legged monkey,' I said, and Brian grinned, always so good-humoured.

'Bananas for tea then?' he asked.

We had pork chops as it happened, with roast potatoes and Brussel sprouts in my best thick gravy. Tired though we were, I wanted to lessen the amount of things we had accumulated in our dining room as soon as possible, so after dinner we began to sort the things we had brought home from Elmwood.

I sat on the living room floor on an old, clean tablecloth to protect the carpet, and opened one of the tan attaché cases; the one containing letters that were to do with Malcolm's death. They made very interesting reading; official letters sent between Uncle Tom and Malcolm's senior officers in the army, where he had been posted for two years' National Service in Reading.

'Brian, come and look at these…'

He joined me on the floor, pulling his reading glasses from the breast pocket of his shirt.

'This is the one I read briefly yesterday,' he said seriously. 'I can't believe this, Mags; it implies that Malcolm was in heavy debt, and owed some senior chap money in the army. This sergeant is implying in the letter that it was the reason he took his life… and by throwing himself under a train, of all things…'

'Oh Bri, how awful!' I took the thin old piece of typed paper, and read the details for myself.

'That's just terrible! Oh, poor Aunt Helen and Uncle Tom!'

'But then, here's Uncle Tom's reply…'

Brian was busy reading another of the letters, and he eventually passed it to me.

'That puts a different slant on the matter,' he said. 'Uncle Tom is saying that Malcolm was under pressure; bullying was, in fact, his word; and that the debt was really someone else's. It seems he was being blackmailed by this sergeant for money to pay off heavy gambling debts, and he just got trapped in a spiral of military bullying.'

'No! That's terrible... he was only, what, nineteen? And probably never away from home before. How would he have been able to stand up to a sergeant like that?'

'I imagine National Service was a real struggle for some blokes in those days.' Brian looked troubled for his cousin. 'And Malcolm broke under the pressure.'

He sighed, and pulled another paper from the case.

'Look, here's a pencilled 'account', if you like, in Uncle Tom's handwriting. He no doubt did this before writing to the authorities after Malcolm's death.'

We read for a while in silence, and then Brian folded the paper and sighed.

'Phew, that was a shocker, love. I'd no idea, you know. No wonder we never talked about it at home...'

It seemed that Uncle Tom had at first given Malcolm money when he came home with an invented story, but of course, the bullying continued. Unknowingly, Uncle Tom gave Malcolm several gifts to help him out at different times, but Malcolm never confided in his father as to what was going on. Bullying, in those days, wasn't talked about; those who were at the receiving end were often considered weak, and Malcolm would have felt ashamed.

Eventually it appeared that Uncle Tom refused to give Malcolm any more money, thinking it was important for his son to stand on his own two feet; though financially, he could easily have continued to help him. At the end of his tether, and under extremely vicious pressure from the sergeant, Malcolm took his own life on the railway line at Reading.

What a story. What a sadness. One's only precious son, unable to bear life any longer at the mercy of an evil superior soldier. How must Tom and Helen have felt? How could they have dealt with such a tragedy, and indeed, how did the man responsible ever live with himself after that?

'Look, here's an old diary, Aunt Helen's, I think.' Brian looked up the date in November 1955, and read the heart-wrenching account of a broken and grieving mother, whose beloved son had not even been able to say goodbye.

For the rest of the year in the diary were entries stating:

'It's ten days/twenty days/five weeks' and so on, 'since I saw Malcolm'; or 'since Malcolm was here at home.'

Aunt Helen's life just seemed to have stopped as well on that terrible November day when Malcolm was pulled dead from beneath a railway train.

Another entry read:

'Tom has been so kind to me.' Which struck me as rather odd. Surely he would be kind, wouldn't he, under such appalling circumstances?

And what of Uncle Tom? Dear, gentle, kind Uncle Tom, who had been the only encouraging, compassionate one to Paul Lench when his mother had died. Uncle Tom, whose refusal of a final gift of money for his son, had indirectly caused his miserable death.

'That explains everything, Mags, I'd say,' said Brian quietly. 'Uncle Tom's 'distance' from the rest of us in the family, possibly especially from Louise and me, who were Malcolm's generation. Their apparent strangeness with us all, you know, both of them, while he was alive. Aunt Helen always said it was the pressure of his work, but now I wonder.'

I removed my glasses and wiped my eyes.

'I feel wretched for him, Bri, I really do. He must have felt so responsible; so much to blame. Of course, he wasn't,' I added quickly. 'How was he to know what Malcolm would do, what pressure he was under, even? No blame on Uncle Tom, none at all... but I bet he felt it all the same, and couldn't forgive himself.'

Brian was very quiet, and he leant back against the sofa, stretching his legs in front of him on the old tablecloth, now littered with letters, envelopes and papers. He fingered Aunt Helen's old diary thoughtfully.

'And what about her?' he said. 'Could she forgive him, do you think? Did she ever forgive him, for losing their only son?'

Chapter Sixteen

The auctioneer's valuer arrived at Elmwood in a hurry, bustled around the rooms listing antiques from amongst the furnishings and effects, and bustled out again as though his life depended on it. As he shot through the front door on his way out, he looked over his shoulder with half a hand raised to Brian in farewell, looking as though a large demon with a forked tail was following him at double his pace.

'Hardly got his name,' Brian commented to me over the phone, 'but he's left me a hand-written list to refer to, and he'll send me a copy of his report to Frank Willis when it's done.'

'Did you say about the clocks?'

'Yes, I did, but he said to refer to Frank on that one. They'll definitely both go to auction. A staggering amount of stuff will, actually; it should raise absolutely thousands. Things you and I would never have considered worth a bean...'

I found it hard to answer this, feeling the injustice of it all for Brian, and Louise too.

'I'm on my way home shortly,' he said. 'Oh, by the way... Trevor's still here!' There was a smile in his voice.

'What's he doing, now the cats have all gone?'

'Well, I suspect he may have wanted to know about the antiques and their value,' Brian suggested quietly, as he was speaking on his mobile at the house.

'He appeared from his room when Joe Bloggs arrived—'

'That's never his name!' I interrupted.

'No; I just can't remember it; well, Trevor just joined us, would you believe, and came round the house with us as though he owned it all!'

'Did he gather what value was put on each item?' I asked suspiciously.

Brian laughed.

'Oh yes, he didn't miss a thing, that was obvious. And then he disappeared upstairs again. I think that's why he came back, you know; he must have heard that the valuer was coming. I dare say it was just a tale about his new place not being ready for a few days.'

'Well, darling, you ought to let Frank know... just in case anything goes missing.'

'There's no sign of the green van...'

'All the same; it could be parked round the corner or something.'

'Mags, what can we do about it, anyway? It's not our problem, honestly.'

Frank Willis kindly agreed to honour Aunt Helen's wish that the two clocks should remain in our family. Sadly, they were both too tall to look right in our modern homes, so Brian and Louise decided to sell them at auction with the rest of the antiques, but the sale price for these would come to them rather than the Cats' Charity.

'It's not much as a total inheritance,' I commented. 'Just think how much money Aunt Helen has already given to the charity; all her investments, bank accounts and so forth, let alone these antiques. And then there's Elmwood, and all the land... it must be worth an absolute fortune, rolled into one.'

Brian sighed.

'Well over a couple of million pounds, I'd say,' he estimated. 'But there we are, Mags. Can't be helped. That old saying "Money is the root of all evil" certainly rings true for us, doesn't it? It was the cause of Malcolm's death, for sure.'

I was quiet, pondering Brian's comment. Such a wise man, and calm and honest too. How many people, I wondered, would be so accepting of such an unjust situation, especially if they were struggling so desperately for cash as we were that year? I had just sold some of my family treasures, to see us through; things I had never wanted to part with, of great sentimental value, but we had no choice other than to sell them to pay the wages for Andrew's staff at the gym. The sale of the business was proving harder by far than expected, and there had been no sensible offers at all. We were really fearful for the future, both for Andrew and Mary, and ourselves. It was indeed, incredibly hard to see all the family antiques removed from Elmwood to benefit the Cats' Charity even further. I hoped that we would never get to the point of being glad of a tin of pilchards or sardines ourselves.

★

Lesley phoned on a Friday.

'Maggie, I'm ringing in distress,' she said, sounding weary.

'James is away with the rowing boys on an international training camp, and Emily and Lauren have both got a tummy bug. There's sick everywhere... can you come?'

I'm not a fair-weather granny, more of a 'hands-on' one, come rain or shine, sickness or smiles.

'I'll be with you in an hour,' I said, mentally organising Brian's meals, and dog care at home, in case I was away for a few days.

'Crikey, Mags, suppose you go down with it too?' Brian said anxiously, as I packed my bag with pyjamas, washing things and the essential Angelina Ballerina books from my Granny box.

'Oh nonsense, do I ever?' I huffed. 'I've lost count of the sickly children I've had and I seldom caught a thing.'

'Well, take care, my darling. And don't bring anything back here,' he added ruefully.

I set off to Bedford in my car, leaving lists of instructions at home. The last time I was away from Brian overnight he cooked peas for his dinner from the frozen bag reserved for sprains and injuries in the freezer. It had been there for several years, but he said afterwards that the peas had tasted excellent. I promised to phone often to report on the girls' progress.

Just over an hour later I pulled into the drive, sad to notice that no excited little girls were jumping up and down in the doorway as usual, to welcome me. I used my key and let myself in. The house was abnormally quiet.

'Is that you, Maggie?' a weary voice called from the bedroom. 'We're all up here... I've got it too, now.'

Two at a time up the stairs, and I found Lesley lying on her bed, pale and poorly, with Emily nestling in the crook of her arm.

'Oh no, love, not all of you at once! Never mind, I'm here to help. Now, what's to be done?'

'Lauren's asleep in her room. She feels awfully hot, but she hasn't been sick for a while.'

Emily sat up, hugging her beloved Bagpuss.

'I have Granny,' she said. 'Lots.'

I smoothed the long, wavy brown hair away from her pale little face, and sat beside them both on the bed.

'Poor darling. Never mind, soon be better. I brought my 'Angelina' books for poorly girls.'

Her little face cheered slightly. Angelina Ballerina was a favourite; a little dancing mouse whose stories were a delight.

'Did you bring the video too, Granny?' asked our small invalid, and I was able to nod that I had.

'Now, Lesley, what shall I do first? Do you want a drink?' I asked.

Lesley moaned at the thought.

'Ooh no, not yet. But... do you mind... there's a pile of sicky sheets and things to wash from the girls in the night. Out on the landing, I'm afraid...'

'Not to worry, I'll do them in a jiffy. Emily, shall we leave Mummy to rest a bit, and I'll read to you on your bed for a while?'

Emily wriggled off the bed and we left Lesley to sleep. Having checked on little Lauren, whose flushed little cheeks and shiny blonde curls were peeping over her sheet, I saw that she was still sleeping peacefully, and we went into Emily's room together. The three of us, Bagpuss included, curled up on the pink fairy duvet for a story.

As I washed sheets and pyjamas, and found fish in the freezer for a simple tea, I thought that this was a far cry from Elmwood and the squalor and degradation of the situation there. What a joy our two little ones were, even when they were ill, and how lucky I felt to have them.

Two days later, Lesley had recovered and both girls were playing merrily in their playhouse in the garden, when James returned from the rowing camp.

'Thanks, Mum,' he said, giving me a hug. Tall and tanned from being abroad, strong arms around me and a broad grin; I felt proud of the man he had become.

'Daddy! Daddy!'

Two little girls hugging his legs, thrilled to have him home. 'We've been poorly! What have you brought us?'

James squatted down to talk to his daughters, one perching on each knee, with arms around his neck.

'I was sick, Daddy, and there were baked beans in it,' volunteered Lauren.

'Me too! Lots of times… and Mummy,' added Emily. 'I didn't go to school. Or gym club,' she remembered sadly.

Lesley joined us all in the garden, pulling her cardigan close around her, still feeling weak. James stood to hug her.

'Wondered where you were,' he mumbled into her hair.

'I was having a bath,' she smiled, 'and I heard you pull up outside. Sorry. Had to get dry and dressed before I could come down.'

'You look rather pale still, love…'

'Oh, I'm heaps better, thanks to your Mum. She's been wonderful.'

I left after dinner… fish fingers with mashed potatoes and jelly to follow; and drove thankfully home to London, glad that I was leaving one well little family behind.

I didn't realise what I would discover on my return.

Chapter Seventeen

'I'm home!'

Two excited dogs running to be petted, with tails wagging to greet me, and Brian hurrying into the hall from his office, arms wide for a welcome hug. It was good to be back and to be together again, even though I had only been away for three days. Brian and I were seldom apart, and we functioned better when we were together, or so we like to think.

He made tea and I unpacked my bag, and produced the pictures drawn for Grandpa, which were to be stuck on the wall in his office. Having given Brian the family news and reported favourably on the recovery to health situation in the Bedford household, I took a deep breath and relaxed into my favourite armchair with my mug of tea in both hands.

'So tell me your news,' I said. 'Any more from Elmwood since I went? Is Trevor still there?'

Brian shook his head.

'I think he's gone again,' he said, yawning. 'I was there yesterday and there was no sign of him.'

'Did you... um... check around? You know, to see if anything's missing since the valuer's visit?'

He grinned.

'I did not, Maggie,' he said severely, and I knew that Brian, with his generous and honest nature, would not have wanted to discover discrepancies that he couldn't prove.

'I tell you what, though, the place was overrun with Cats' Charity people. They came to fetch furniture that isn't going to auction; stuff they think they can clean up and sell. There were tables and chairs going in and out and boxes of this and that... a whole house clearance job, really. Four of them on the job and a fair-sized van.'

'Beryl and Sally?'

'Uh-huh. And two blokes; a big guy with the muscles called Ken and a nice little chap called Dave, who brought in lunch from the fish and chip shop, and made lists all day.'

I seemed to have missed quite an event, and I wondered whether the house would soon be sorted, and put up for sale.

'Brian, what about the rest of Gordon's old stuff?' I asked, finishing my tea and moving to sit on the floor at his feet, with my elbow on his knees. He massaged my neck.

'Well, that's what I was tackling yesterday in fact,' he said. 'When I finished work here at lunchtime, I went straight to Elmwood and got going again on Gordon's study in Malcolm's old room, because the Cats people wouldn't be touching those things. I did the rest of the filing cabinet and the desk drawers, and I unearthed quite a find…'

'What sort of a find?'

Brian stood up and I followed him into the dining room, where we had stacked the boxes and attaché cases brought home previously, that were to be kept. There were three in all, with precious letters and papers still to be read. On the table in the far corner was an old biscuit tin, large and square, with 'McVites Family Assortment' on the lid.

'Look at these,' Brian said, lifting the lid, and out tumbled more letters and birthday-type cards, onto the table. I found my glasses and set to work at the table beside Brian, reading the contents of this correspondence with renewed interest. Some of it had not been touched, I thought, for at least fifty years.

Virtually all the letters and cards were sent to Gordon by Aunt Helen. There were tiny tags from presents, signed:

'To a dear friend, from Helen.'

'To dear Gordon, with love, Helen.'

I was puzzled.

'Why on earth would he have kept all these?' I said, and Brian raised one eyebrow.

'Read on,' he said quietly.

There were old-fashioned birthday cards; I guessed of around the late 1950s, with handwritten messages from Helen to Gordon, sounding a good deal more affectionate than we would have expected. I read aloud:

'I am thinking of you today, dear Gordon, and wishing you happiness and contentment in our deep friendship. With my eternal love, Helen.'

Another read:

'Sincere wishes for your birthday Gordon, and as you possess such determination to overcome difficulties I am sure the future still has happiness to hand you in our very great friendship. I am here to help you along through bleak patches.

My dearest love to you always, Helen.'

The postmark on that envelope was dated 1952.

I looked up at Brian, aghast.

'And that's not all,' he said, passing me one fat envelope containing more recent notes and cards. 'Take a look in here.'

As I read what were clearly love letters of a genteel nature, it became obvious that Aunt Helen's feelings for Gordon Lench were far more affectionate than we had ever known. Indeed, it would seem that their relationship had begun in such a way right back in the 1950s, possibly around the time of Gordon's wife's early death, but certainly before Malcolm's. From what we read in the letters, Helen had initially written offering loving support when Gordon's wife became ill with some serious disease and needed surgery, and subsequently when he was widowed; but even then the tone of her writing was far more familiar than one would expect of a mere neighbour, even a close one.

There was a printed poem, cut out of a magazine or book, which read:

> 'The gift of sympathy is never spent
> Or lost forever.
> Love that is lent ungrudgingly to ease
> Another's pain
> Comes back again, Heaven sent,
> To rest in peace upon the giver.'

And it was signed:

'Love always my darling, Helen.'

I was shocked, and looked at Brian to see his reaction too.

'Bri, none of these cards for birthdays or Christmas, or the present tags and so forth… none of them is from Uncle Tom as well as Aunt Helen. Just her. Isn't that odd?'

He cleared his throat, as if feeling uncomfortable.

'Not if she sent them secretly,' he said, 'and judging by the messages, I think she must have done.'

I had found another.

'Look, here's a New Year's card dated 1953. There's a verse:

> New Year's Day might well be named
> The day of Auld Lang Syne,
> Because it adds another year to
> Friendship; yours and mine!
>
> Love always sweetheart, Helen.

'Oh, Bri…'

I looked up at him and removed my glasses. 'Poor Uncle Tom.'

'Quite a revelation, eh? And a mystery too,' he added. 'We're just assuming something here…'

'But darling, why on earth would old Gordon have kept all these letters and things like treasures, if he didn't feel the same? There must have been a real love affair going on between them, don't you think?'

'Well yes, it looks like it, though just these letters alone isn't enough evidence really.'

I dug around in the biscuit tin, and tied tightly with string was a thin pile of envelopes, all blue, all written in Aunt Helen's handwriting. I held it out to Brian.

'Should we?'

'In for a penny, in for a pound,' he said, standing up to fetch the scissors from my sewing box by the sideboard. He cut the string, gingery dust from it falling like powder onto the floor. 'We've come this far…'

Brian read aloud four letters, disclosing without any doubt a very passionate love affair between Aunt Helen and Gordon. These letters were dated in the late 1960s, many years before Uncle Tom died in 1982. Did he, we wondered, ever know what was going on between his beloved wife and his so-called friend next door? Indeed, did Brian's parents know, or even suspect? Had Auntie Pearl known, too? It was impossible to tell, and now that they were all gone, we would never find out.

Could this, I wondered, be the reason there was a chill between them all, a cool distance maintained by Uncle Tom to avoid any questions being asked? And did they all pretend that the reason was really Malcolm's death, and the sadness that ensued, so as to mask the real cause?

While we were cogitating, the phone rang, sounding extra loud in the silence of the dining room. We realised that we had been sitting in the stillness, so absorbed by the letters that we weren't aware of the time. The early evening light was beginning to fade, and we hadn't had our meal.

'You go, I'll get dinner,' I said, jumping up. Brian answered the phone, and chatted for a while to Louise while I rummaged through the fridge for leftovers to cook at speed.

We ate omelettes, watching the BBC news, but our conversation continually returned to the letters. Such a discovery; did we want to tell the family? Would it be best to keep it all to ourselves, so long after it had all happened?

Strangely, it was only two days later that a girl called Janet from the BBC documentary department telephoned, and asked Brian whether he would agree to a programme being made about Elmwood, and in particular, Aunt Helen and Uncle Tom.

'I'm sorry... I don't understand why you're calling, really,' Brian said. 'How did you get hold of my phone number?'

'From Trevor Hill, Mr Fawley,' Janet informed him.

'You remember the eviction case a month or so ago, and the news coverage of it all on the BBC...?'

'I do indeed.'

Brian was beginning to understand.

Janet went on:

'Well, I actually asked Mr Hill at the time... I came to the house you see, to get the footage for the evening news;... but he referred me to you as the family member to contact.'

'Why would you want to run a programme about Elmwood? Or my aunt and uncle? He's been dead for twenty odd years now...'

'Oh yes, I know, Mr Fawley, but what a gentleman he was. I've already found out loads about him and his wife. I just got a really good feeling that day about doing a programme, because the house is so interesting. Could I come and talk to you about doing a documentary in the autumn?'

Brian coughed, unsure of the wisdom of such a thing, especially as we had uncovered things we would not wish to be publicised on television.

'No... I'm sorry, Janet, I think not.'

'Oh, but Mr Fawley! It would make a wonderful programme! Trevor Hill told me a thing or two; as a family friend, you know; and I'm sure the whole story is much more interesting—'

'Like I said, Janet,' Brian interrupted, beginning to feel angry, 'I'm afraid not. In fact, most definitely not. Goodbye.'

We were annoyed with Trevor for implying to the media that he was a family friend, as it wasn't at all true; and in particular that he had disclosed sufficient details of the lives of Uncle Tom and Aunt Helen to cause this Janet so much interest.

Having uncovered secrets ourselves, we wondered what Trevor also, had found, as we felt certain that nothing in the house had been left unturned by him during his stay.

'Oh well, Mags, too late to worry now. Trevor's gone. What a to-do, eh?'

Dear Brian, always so accepting. I knew, however, that he was anxious. We continued to go to Elmwood at least twice a week, usually more, until the sorting and clearing was complete.

We never dreamed at that stage, that we had only just begun to unearth a mystery greater than we could have imagined.

Chapter Eighteen

'Mags! Mags! Are you up here? Can you hear me?'

Brian shouted from the loft, and I was down on the first floor landing, by Aunt Helen's room. I hurried up to him, through the access door at the very top of the house, and into the storage section of the loft space. The loft itself was easily reached from the very top floor of the house, where Trevor Hill had made the old servants' quarters his home. This gave direct access to the outer loft space without needing a ladder, as would be the case in smaller modern houses. From this ante-room we could enter the loft by climbing over a small ledge into the loft itself.

I have never liked spiders, and the creatures to be found in here had been growing undisturbed, for thirty or more years. It was like something out of a horror film, and I steeled myself to pass the cobwebs and make my way into the actual loft space where Brian was searching through the contents.

'What is it? Are you OK?'

Bravely, I brushed a thick cobweb from my face with a shudder. Brian held a large torch, but there was natural light coming through the roof as well, where repairs were in serious need.

'God, Bri, I thought you were trapped or something...'

He held out a hand to steady me as I picked my way carefully across the rafters. The loft was very old and unboarded, and in a state of appalling disrepair. Because of the number of holes in the roof, not only light came in; the loft contents were largely damp from incoming rain and snow over the years, and also extremely dirty.

'Be careful, darling... miss a beam and you will go through the ceiling and end up downstairs,' Brian warned me scarily.

'Why did you yell? Oh Lord, I hate it up here!'

'Look at this!'

Brian's 'find' was a small trunk, the lid of which he had already opened. In his torchlight, and disregarding spiders and decades of dust, I could tell that the contents were personal treasures from many years ago; baby clothes wrapped in fine paper, piles of letters tied in faded ribbon, furled certificates and old photographs... some in frames, some in albums, and some loose and curling at the edges. There were sporting medals and an envelope containing old school reports. And a number of termly batels (accounts) from Brasenose College, Oxford, between 1927 and 1929.

'Can you help me pull this out of the loft?' Brian asked keenly. This trunk had obviously belonged to Uncle Tom, and it held some family history. Delighted as I was that he had found it, I didn't share his enthusiasm for lifting it, and thereby disturbing the many beasties, which I suspected, lay beneath.

'Hmph! Are you prepared to take responsibility for my nervous breakdown?' I said apprehensively. 'I don't like the look of the probable inhabitants of this thing...'

'Oh, for heaven's sakes, Mags, get a grip. It's only the odd spider or two... here, there's a handle at each end.'

Brian closed the lid and clouds of filthy dust blew into our faces. I spluttered, wiping my eyes with my sleeve, and an already dirty hand.

'Let's just get out of here...'

'Lift it carefully, now... mind where you put your feet...'

All around us, now that my eyes had adjusted to the half-light, I could see relics of the early days at Elmwood for Uncle Tom and Aunt Helen. It was like stepping back in time...

There was some old garden furniture, '30s style, canvas director chairs and an old, crumbling canvas sun umbrella. Several tennis rackets with broken strings and old wooden handles lay in a sorry heap. A few rolls of what was probably old carpet, wrapped in brown paper and tied with string, blocked our way. Even an old-fashioned wooden highchair, with small metal wheels at the bottom of its legs, lay resting on its side; little faded blue teddy bears painted around the edge of its tray.

I stumbled over some rusted paint tins, and saw to my horror, an enamel bucket in which lived an extremely large black spider with long, hairy legs. I was even unable to scream. Piles and piles of old books were heaped in one corner of the loft, tied together in varying numbers, with old whiskery string.

'Everything is tied with string,' I commented. 'They must have used absolutely balls of it.'

'Before the days of Sellotape,' said Brian, puffing under the weight of the trunk. He was taking the majority of it, and wielding the torch in one hand.

'Loads of old newspapers over here in piles,' I said.

'Look where you're going!'

'I am. Don't shout.'

As we moved towards the door to the loft space I spotted another small tan attaché case, lying at a rakish angle against the wall, as if it had been thrown up here at random. It was similar to those we had found downstairs in the study, and we picked it up and took it with us for investigation.

We managed to lift the old trunk out of the access space and onto the top landing, where I could see properly, to my horror, the thick cobwebs and grime of so many years, covering the outer casing. Brian wiped the old brass nameplate... 'THOMAS FAWLEY'.

'This was probably a university trunk. I don't think he ever went to boarding school,' he said.

'Well, what are we going to do with it now?' I asked, afraid that Brian might want to take the whole thing home.

To my relief he said:

'Let's empty it into those big plastic storage boxes; they're in the car, I'll get them. And then we'll go through all this at home; the stuff inside isn't too dirty, Mags, it's been well sealed.'

He read my mind. Our home was fast becoming cluttered with old treasures in the form of letters, biscuit tins and photographs, and Easter was on the way, when all the family would be coming to stay.

'Well, we must sort it quickly,' I said firmly. 'We can't leave all those piles of things in the dining room for too long, with everyone coming in a couple of weeks.'

'Righto, I promise.'

He went down the stairs two at a time to fetch the boxes, carrying the little tan case, and I went to clean my dirty, streaked face.

★

It was almost April, and the daffodils appeared as if by magic, their yellow trumpets facing the sun to herald the spring.

As we drove home that day with so much history behind us in the boot, I felt as though the year was running ahead without us and we were trapped in time gone by, at Elmwood. Every day the house was uncovering stories for us, and as we pieced them together, the mystery unfolded.

That afternoon, we spread the old tablecloth once more on the floor at home, and set to work with mugs of coffee, to discover Uncle Tom.

'Wow. Quite an achiever, wasn't he?'

Brian was elbow-deep in school reports and details of sports achievements. Uncle Tom, it seemed, had done it all; won everything, passed all his exams, and eventually been awarded an exhibition to Oxford University. At Brasenose College he gained a first class degree in physics, was head of societies, captain of sports teams, and won a 'blue' for boxing. Was there anything, I wondered, that he didn't do, or achieve? No surprise really, that he went on to be awarded a knighthood in later life. And yet despite all this, he died a saddened man, and his place was filled in Aunt Helen's heart by a rogue so much less worthy.

'Bri, look at these baby things.'

I held up tiny vests with satin ribbons, yellowed with age and once knitted in the finest of wool, with love. There were romper suits with buttoned flaps at the back to enable nappy changing. Of the old terry towelling kind, of course, long before the days of disposables.

'These must have been Malcolm's.'

'Or the twins' before him,' Brian added, remembering the baby boys who had died early in the marriage.

There was a faded pale blue pram rug with an appliquéd rabbit in the corner, and some beautiful tiny nightdresses in fine white lawn, with frilled cuffs and pleated bodices.

'Girly, really,' I said, 'but in those days boys wore gowns as well as girls, didn't they?'

An obvious christening gown was carefully folded in paper, with crumbling tissue between the layers of the long skirt.

'This is so beautiful. Probably a family one, and no one has worn it since Malcolm. Maybe too sad...'

We carefully sorted the treasures into piles, some to keep for posterity, but most to discard, sadly, for lack of space or need to retain them.

'Here's a photo album of their courtship days I should think,' said Brian, while I lingered over baby wear; charmed by it all but sad that none of the occupants of these beautiful, tiny clothes had survived beyond youth at best.

'Look at these pictures, Mags... they seemed so happy. These are taken at the tennis club where they met; and these on a holiday, I guess.'

There was one special letter, so youthful and happy, from Tom to Helen in their very early days. The postmark was dated 1928, and they would both have been twenty-one years old. It was written in black ink, on a beige coloured paper, and the address at the top of the letter was the Fawley family home in Wimbledon. It read:

Dear Helen,

I shall be quite free tomorrow afternoon, so if you haven't fixed anything, our proposed outing stands. We should have discussed arrangements last night, but as we didn't, I hope the suggestions I am going to make will be all right. I will, I really will think out a programme and since it will most probably necessitate starting from the station, I think it would be best if I met you there. If I were to call for you at East Sheen I think things would get a bit late. I will be at the District Railway Station at Wimbledon at 2.20. If you can't get there as early as that, never mind; a little waiting won't hurt me. I'm used to it. (this is not meant to be rude.) Let us pray that the weather calms down a bit.

Last night was my lucky night with regard to buses and trains, as I got both without any delay at all. One amusing thing, constituting an awful warning (!) happened on the bus. As we were passing Barnes Common a man and a girl got on the bus. The man sat beside me on the other side of the gangway. His back was covered with grass. A cheery looking old man sitting behind him winked at me and burst out into loud laughter, but I managed to suppress my mirth more successfully. The girl had a few bits of grass in her hair.

Nothing else to write about, most precious, except that I seemed to dream of you all night, and hope to do so again in a few hours' time.

Cheerio, my dear,

Love Tom.

We stopped our pondering over the trunk contents late that evening, the two dogs impatient for a last walk, and our supper dishes unwashed in the sink. I felt weary; drained emotionally, and Brian too, was very tired. He took the dogs out briefly while I cleared the kitchen before bed.

'George! Millie! Come on; last walk time, boys. Find your leads.'

The door banged and they were gone.

My mind refused to relax, and I slept fitfully all night, constantly waking as if I had been dreaming too busily. The early dawn crept through the curtains, and I heard rain on the window panes. Brian snored loudly beside me, a sure sign that he too, was not completely relaxed in sleep. We rose to the new day tired, and Brian as usual, made the morning tea.

He pulled the bedroom curtains.

'Foul day.'

I yawned.

'I heard the rain in the night. It's windy, too. There were no birds singing at dawn this morning.'

'What are your plans today?'

We sipped our tea in bed, and turned on the television for the news. I shrugged, plan free for a change.

'Nothing special; laundry for the gym, things like that. And you?'

'Busy today, love; working in the office all morning at least.'

'Not going to Elmwood again then, this afternoon? We've still got a fair bit to finish.'

'No, I can't spare the time today. The house will have to wait, I think.'

Once we were dressed and breakfasted, I searched for my handbag to go shopping. Normally on the low cupboard in the hall, it was not in its usual place.

'Do you remember bringing it home last night?' Brian asked, and I thought back to the excitement of the trunk, and boxing the contents and driving home intent on an immediate bath after our sortie to the loft.

'No… I don't, actually. I think it may still be in the hall at Elmwood. Oh damn! I'll have to drive over for it…'

'Shame. Nuisance for you; sorry I can't go, but I must work… loads to do.'

Brian was opening a pile of work mail, and I could see he was already mentally in office mode. I kissed him goodbye and headed off through the rain in my car. It was, by now, almost on automatic pilot to Elmwood, so used to the route were we.

It was a bad morning, weather-wise, and the spring daffodils under the trees in the woodland garden at Elmwood looked weary, bent low as they were, against the rain. The wind lashed spray against the windows, and a Tesco carrier bag blew around the front porch, having escaped from the rubbish sacks by the gate.

I hurried inside, cursing Trevor for his wooden barricade which made entry to the house more awkward. Gone were the printed signs, and the papers stuck up everywhere with scrawled threats to any entrants. Gone too, was the mew of welcome that Coco had given us every time we had called before. The house was as silent and cold as the grave.

Most of the furniture of little value had been taken now, polished and for sale in the charity shop; and only the antiques for auction remained. A date for their collection had been arranged for one week after Easter, and before that Brian and I had to ensure that all the drawers of those items were empty.

With relief I located my handbag in Aunt Helen's bedroom, and was about to leave when a massive clap of thunder shook the house. I decided to wait until the storm had lessened, to avoid having to run to the car in torrential rain.

A good opportunity, I thought, to empty the chest of drawers while I waited, so I set to work with a large rubbish sack and began from the bottom, deepest drawer.

Jumpers, cardigans, a badly deteriorated fur stole, and gloves… dozens of them. Long evening gloves, short leather gloves, tiny lace afternoon tea gloves from so many years ago. A dank, old and rotten smell pervaded the drawer, and I decided nothing was worth keeping for any purpose, so I scooped it all into the sack, just checking as I did so for any hidden jewellery boxes. Nothing.

The next drawer held underwear, nightdresses, bed-jackets and stockings, all size 'small'. Everything went into the sack.

One more drawer from the top, a shallower one this time, held scarves and handkerchiefs in satin pouches, some jewelled evening bags and velvet purses on gilt chains. Narrow leather belts, to fit such a tiny waist, were at the back of the drawer… and as I pulled them out, I saw the boxes.

I opened an old chocolate box, once a fancy folding one for Terry's All Gold, and discovered with a sigh… yet more letters. These seemed to be random ones, some from friends after evenings spent together, some from family after Uncle Tom's death, but none appeared to be intimately personal.

Another box, this time smaller, with a picture of swans on the lid. It held diaries, small handbag-sized ones, and notebooks.

The last box, nearer the front of the drawer and easily visible, held an assortment of cards from Christmases past and birthdays, postcards from holidays and letters in envelopes, largely, I recognised at once, from our family. Some were from Louise, and some, in our children's youthful handwriting, were thank-you notes after their birthdays. All had been sent to Aunt Helen over the years after Uncle Tom died, when our relationship with her had deepened. Most of the cards depicted kittens, or cats.

Interestingly, there was no sign of the considerable number of notes, cards and letters we had sent in the last year of Aunt Helen's life, when we seldom saw her because of her illness, and latterly, when Gordon severed all contact due to the TB. I wondered what had become of all of those.

The top two drawers, one on each side of the chest, held cosmetics, silver-backed brushes, talcum powder and trinkets. The empty jewellery boxes remained, and I was reminded of Trevor Hill. There was a box of dozens of the dangling type of earrings, always favoured by Aunt Helen, and fake pearls, bead necklaces and dress rings, all of no real value.

I put this collection to one side in a Sainsbury's box for the ladies at the charity shop, but I carefully carried the chocolate boxes downstairs to take home for perusal.

As I did so, handbag over my shoulder this time so as not to forget it again, I almost jumped out of my skin. Someone was in the house, and I could hear heavy footfalls in the hallway.

'Woo hoo! Is that you, Maggie?'

With relief I recognised Sally from the Cats' Charity, this time wearing a rather wet navy anorak, and as usual, smoking a cigarette. As she spoke, it wobbled up and down in the corner of her mouth.

'I've come to read the meters,' she said. 'Terrible day.'

'Sally! You gave me a fright. It's quite creepy, being here alone.'

I explained about my handbag.

'Mmm… can't say I mind. I'm doing this sort of thing in old houses all the time,' Sally said, 'but not many are as gruesome as this one!' She laughed. 'I certainly can't understand why that Trevor bod wanted to stay here on his own. Finally gone now, has he?'

I hesitated to say for certain, as already Trevor had returned once to our knowledge since he bade us farewell originally.

Sally read the meters, made a note on her clipboard, and we left Elmwood together. The rain had virtually stopped, and just a fine drizzle hung in the air. I was glad the wind had dropped, and we stood by our cars chatting before driving our separate ways away down Gumber Lane.

Chapter Nineteen

The day before Good Friday arrived, and Brian and I drove our final load of documents, papers and boxes home from Elmwood to be checked. Nothing of any importance remained as far as we could tell; drawers and cupboards were empty and bags were sorted. Sack loads of rubbish had been removed to the nearest waste disposal site, but the poor house still looked a shambles.

Brian worked in his office late into the evening, finalising as far as was possible at that stage, everything for probate in respect of Gordon's estate.

At ten o'clock I made a pot of tea and took it on a tray with two mugs into the office to join him. The computer hummed, and the desk lamp illuminated piles of old papers neatly sorted, checked and recorded.

'I don't ever want to be an executor,' I said, pouring tea.

'Hmm; no chance of that, I'd say darling... I think you'll be quite safe in that direction.' Brian laughed, referring to my total lack of financial know-how or ability. We drank our tea.

Sitting staring at me was the old briefcase Brian had brought from Gordon's study. It was open, as he had just been searching in it for relevant documents. I could see some loose old photographs poking out of one section, so I pulled them out to have a look.

In one, Gordon as a young man, clearly recognisable, stared back at me. Alongside him was obviously his family, lined up on a beach somewhere, probably on holiday. His mother, short and stout; his father in shirt sleeves and braces, with his trousers rolled up to the knees; a younger brother, and a large, unattractive girl I presumed was his sister.

'He was quite a good-looking young fellow, wasn't he?' I said, showing Brian the photo. He peered at it, muttered:

'Not bad, I suppose,' and then, 'Better than this effort on the end. Who do you suppose she is? Obviously last in the line for the beauty handouts, bless her.'

I smiled.

'There's a definite resemblance. Gordon's sister, I'd say; but you're right, she's no picture postcard.'

And then it dawned on me... a lightning flash of recollection... I remembered Paul's revelation on the day he collected his train set from Elmwood.

('My father wasn't my father, and my mother was my aunt.')

'Bri! That's her! Paul's real mother,' I exclaimed, explaining what I had remembered from my conversation with Paul.

'Good Lord! Quite a to-do, eh? No wonder she 'didn't know' who the father was,' Brian grinned mischievously. 'It must have been pretty dark at the time!'

I laughed, but my mind was busy, hurrying on ahead to my next horrific suggestion.

'God, Bri... you don't think...'

I looked hard at the picture again, and yes, Paul did indeed resemble Gordon quite dramatically.

'I know people often do look like their uncles, but... what if Gordon was actually Paul's real father? You know, a case of incest? And maybe that's why Gordon married Florrie, just to be able to adopt his sister's child, because he was responsible, after all?'

Brian scratched his chin, a gesture he so often made when he felt awkward or uncomfortable. This was not a pleasant assumption, and he was being cautious in his response.

'Darling, you can't go saying things like that! I really don't think—' I cut him short.

'Seriously, Bri, joking aside, this Audrey, Gordon's sister, is not a pretty sight. Maybe she never had any boyfriends, and it would have been a terrible scandal if it came out that her own brother—'

'Where's that case?'

Brian stretched to reach the briefcase from which the photo had come, and began to search through the rest of the contents.

'Look, here are some registration certificates... let's see...'

We found a marriage certificate for Gordon and Florence, for a wedding which took place in 1936, just shortly before Paul was born. They must have adopted him soon after, too soon to have been trying unsuccessfully for a child of their own; making me wonder whether the very reason for their marriage, on Gordon's part anyway, was to establish acceptable parents for his son. Paul's adoption would obviously have avoided the shame for Audrey, for being a single mother in those days was indeed a disgrace.

There was of course, nothing to prove Paul's real parentage. I found a small birth certificate for him (why did he not hold this himself?), which stated that his birth had been registered in 1953, when he would have been seventeen years old. It was one of the shortened versions, not stating names of either parent, and I wondered whether it had been obtained then just before National Service, which necessitated a copy.

We sat quietly, horrified at our discovery, and I slowly replaced the photographs and certificates in their compartments in the briefcase.

Easter came and went amid a flurry of family meals, an Easter egg hunt in our large garden, and church on the Sunday. To my delight we all lined up, twelve of us in total in our long pew, and sang the Easter hymns lustily.

Emily and Lauren, used to Sunday School at home, behaved beautifully. Before the sermon they went to the crèche with Lesley, to paint Easter bunnies and make paper crosses on a hill to take home. Lauren was a little confused.

'The Easter bunny is called Jesus,' she told me, skipping along afterwards, holding my hand on the way to our car. In her other hand was her egg box model of a hillside, painted green, with three paper crosses stuck on the top, blowing in the breeze.

'And this is the hill where all the other bunnies live.'

'No, silly!' Emily gave her a gentle push. 'Jesus wasn't an Easter bunny... he died, Lauren, and went to heaven on a cross to live with Great Grandad.'

Wonderful, I thought, vowing to myself to write all these things down in my 'Granny book' when I had the time.

Our weekend was splendid, and we enjoyed every minute with the family, never giving Elmwood and the unfolding mystery there a single thought.

Well, almost.

It was Easter Sunday evening. We had enjoyed our egg hunt in the garden, followed by a barbecue tea... first of the season, and possible because of excellent weather… and two sleepy little girls had been bathed and 'storied' and tucked up in bed.

Andrew and Mary said their farewells and raced off home to Wimbledon in their blue sports car, the hole in their exhaust causing enough noise to alert the entire neighbourhood to their departure as they sped down the road.

Lucy and Daniel, living nearer, decided to stay a little longer to spend the last of the evening with us all, and Lesley and James were staying overnight again, and taking the girls home on the Monday.

We relaxed in the sitting room, and Brian poured us beers and gin and tonic to aid recovery after a busy day.

'Any crisps, Mum? Or peanuts? I'll get them…'

'In the cupboard, Lucy… usual place. Thanks, darling.'

'Who's for Pictionary?'

James came in with the box, having discovered it in his old room while putting Emily to bed.

'Look at this… when did we last play this one?'

We chuckled at some of the old drawings left in the box from childhood days, and James and Lucy argued jovially about games gone by.

Daniel and Lesley, both 'only' children, shared none of these sibling experiences with anyone, and I watched them exchanging mystified glances, and smiled to myself.

'Come on, everyone; we all have to play.'

Ever the organiser, Lucy distributed the pencils, and Brian returned with our drinks.

We enjoyed the end of the evening and made our weary way to bed, having seen Lucy and Daniel off with food supplies of leftovers for the week ahead, or so it seemed.

Lesley and James had already gone up to the loft bedroom as we turned out all the lights and settled the dogs for the night.

Tired but not sleepy, I fell under the duvet with Brian, but I found it hard to drift off. Dreams eluded me; I tossed and turned, and listened to the night sounds of a house at rest.

At 3 a.m. I was still wide awake, thinking. Thinking about the children, the family, the waning business and our uncertain future. And thinking of Aunt Helen, Uncle Tom, poor Malcolm, and… Gordon Lench.

I crept out of bed, feeling for my fluffy slippers in the dark and pulling on my dressing gown that hung in the shadows behind the bedroom door.

Brian didn't stir; low, gentle snoring sounds coming from his side of the duvet. I crept along the landing, past the girls' bedroom doors, and checked on them both as I went illuminated by their glowing nightlights which were nothing more than a glimmer in the skirting board sockets.

Emily slept on her side as usual, her shock of brown curls around her on the pillow like a fan. She clutched Bagpuss, one leg in her pink 'princess' pyjamas over the top of her duvet.

Little Lauren lay on her back; her baby face angelic in sleep, blonde curls surrounding it like a halo.

Upstairs in the loft room all was still and quiet as James and Lesley slept soundly, and I made my way downstairs to make tea.

The teapot and I were well acquainted at night lately, ever since the serious worries began over Andrew's gym. Our financial situation had worsened so dramatically, and so far there had been no offers on our house, to enable us to raise the money we so desperately needed. Brian seemed able to sleep, but I was less fortunate.

I brewed tea for one in the kitchen, and let Millie out into the garden. As usual, old George remained stretched out in his bed, but Millie was up for a fox-check.

I decided to take my tea into Brian's office, to peruse the old photos once more in Gordon's briefcase. There were several I had not looked at, and other papers besides.

Sitting in the dim light of just the angle-poise lamp at Brian's desk, I sipped my tea and unclicked the catch of the briefcase. It opened to reveal the photos we had seen already, some letters in envelopes, and the registration certificates.

One envelope held family pictures, showing Paul as a baby, as a toddler, and as a small boy. Interestingly, he was almost always with Florence, his adoptive mother; looking happy, seeming loved. Florence was an attractive young woman, always smiling… I was intrigued as to why she and Gordon had never extended their family with children of their own. Then I remembered how in his later years, Gordon always spoke of not liking children at all, and having no time for them and their 'irritating demands.' The photos certainly depicted him as being withdrawn and disinterested in Paul, but he always appeared a happy child in the presence of his mother. And then all that changed when he was sixteen and she died.

I hunted through the certificates for one of Florence's death in 1952, but there wasn't one in the case for her at all. I found one for Audrey Lench, Gordon's sister, who died in 1946 of breast cancer as a young woman, but nothing about Gordon's wife. Odd, I thought, wondering why she had died. Had their marriage been happy, or simply one of convenience, in order to adopt Paul for his sister, and thereby absolve his own guilt? Pure supposition, but it seemed to be horribly possible.

There were photographs too, of an elderly couple with Florence and Gordon, taken in a large leafy garden with a river beyond, and I presumed it to be 'number one' next door. There in the foreground was Paul as a toddler pushing a square-jawed dog on wheels, and laughing happily. This couple I assumed to be Florence's parents, and they appeared to be a good deal more refined than Gordon's mother and father in the previous photograph.

I scrabbled around in the briefcase and found an old typed letter, obviously a carbon copy produced on a typewriter, discussing the purchase of 'number one'. It was written by a solicitor on behalf of Gordon, to a Colonel Bridges who apparently owned the house, and Gordon and Florence were sitting tenants when he wanted to sell it. A transaction took place which enabled the Lenches to purchase 'number one' at a very low price, which I thought explained the old mystery of how a man such as Gordon could ever have afforded such a grand property.

I sipped my tea, intrigued, sleep further from my mind than ever. There was a discrepancy somehow, between the actual and the expected as regarded their marriage. Gordon was an intelligent man, qualified as an electrical engineer, but with a less than classy background. He was born in the East End of London, son of a house painter, and his family was poor. Gordon had never lost his vaguely Cockney accent, which sat ill upon a man living in Gumber Lane. Florence however, known as Florrie, appeared to have been well educated, coming as she did from a good middle-class home where there was money. The picture of her parents indicated that they were 'above' Gordon's in social status, and Florence herself looked more of a lady than Gordon's mother or sister.

When Florence died, Gordon came into money, and decided to buy the house rather than continue to rent. Paul, then sixteen, also inherited some money, and was eventually able to leave home and his abusive father, and make his own way in the world. He and Gordon became estranged, and he was seldom heard of at 'number one', which was no surprise as he was rejected by his father whenever he did make contact.

The story was beginning to come together.

I pushed the photos and papers back into the briefcase and clicked the catch to close it, wondering whether, in fact, my suppositions could all be true. It was all so sadly convincing.

And what then, about Aunt Helen, and Uncle Tom? How were they linked, if at all in those days, to this man who commanded no respect?

I realised that the year Gordon purchased his house next door to Elmwood was the very same year that Malcolm had killed himself on National Service. Could Aunt Helen have needed comfort so desperately then, that she turned to her nearest neighbour, a widower alone, when Uncle Tom's own grief drove him into a shell? Were they unable, like so many couples when tragedy strikes, to comfort one another in their sadness?

Little did I know, as I sat with my tea that night in Brian's office, that there was yet more to be uncovered of this old Elmwood secret, which would add yet another dimension to the mystery.

Chapter Twenty

The Spring brought the rain, and on our more infrequent trips to Elmwood, we noticed how densely overgrown the garden had become. Susie's marked grave was hidden by waist-high weeds which lined the drive on either side. The shrubs were so tall and untended that tendrils brushed our hair and faces as we walked from front gate to front door, reminding me of the magic forest in the children's fairytale of the 'Sleeping Beauty'.

The garden at the back was an undergrowth, the cat shelters now occluded by weeds and tall grasses, and from the house it was almost impossible to see the water's edge by the river.

Still visible, however, was the metal ladder, now entangled with bindweed, propped against the wall between the gardens of the two houses. So many years since Gordon had used it to come secretly to visit Aunt Helen in the days following Uncle Tom's death; and still it stood, reminiscent of the liaison unbeknown to the family, or indeed we assumed, to anyone... even the local neighbours in the lane.

Brian and I disposed of virtually all the boxes and papers we had brought home to sort. We shared the lovely photos with Louise, and sat together reading the wonderful letters of acclaim and congratulations to Uncle Tom on his knighthood in the 1960s.

One of the tan attaché cases held a huge number of invitations to grand occasions; menus and details of social dinners, dances and functions, royal garden parties and élite gatherings, which Uncle Tom and Aunt Helen had attended. Such a 'charmed' lifestyle and so busy; no wonder we as a family had seen so little of them, when Uncle Tom's work had been so important. How little we knew of his involvement in so much; indeed, he had travelled worldwide and was held in great esteem, it seemed, by so many.

A box from his study held special letters; we opened them one early May evening, as we sat with the French windows open onto the patio, enjoying early evening sunshine. The daytime sky had been full of whipped cream clouds scudding along in the breeze. It was somehow difficult to look back at the unfolding story and still be conscious of our place in the present time, as the seasons came and went and the year hurried on by.

'These letters are wonderful, Mags,' Brian said, glasses perched on his nose as he looked up at me over the top with a smile. 'They were happy; really happy. Such loving letters. I never wrote such amazing stuff to you…'

I sighed.

These were letters and cards to Aunt Helen from Uncle Tom when he was away on business, abroad or more locally, but he seemed to write to her frequently from his hotels.

'This one is so gorgeous… he really adored her,' I said, and Brian laughed at the emotion in my voice.

'This is as good as a weepy romantic film, eh, darling?' he smiled. I could always be relied upon to shed a tear over romance in a story.

'Just listen to this,' I continued;

'Missing you my sweetheart more than I can say. I'm longing for my train tomorrow to bring me swiftly to your side.'

How super is that? He was such a romantic, your uncle!'

'Sly old dog,' commented Brian, with a grin.

The letters ranged from the earliest years of their marriage until the middle of the 1950s; probably when things changed between them after Malcolm's death.

Uncle Tom gave accounts of his work, his hotel rooms, the menus and the meals he had eaten both good and bad, and when abroad, details of the cities in which he stayed.

Brian was impressed.

'God knows I'm glad I never had to write to you this often,' he said, and I laughed. Brian was not the most enthusiastic letter-writer; given to short sentences, straight to the point, without detail or emotion. Clearly, this was a gift he had not inherited with his Uncle Tom.

Perhaps this was partly why I was so impressed with the content especially, of the early letters from Tom to Helen. So full of emotion, passion even, and adoration for his young wife. So descriptive and easy to read, written in his small neat handwriting. I felt that he wrote from the heart, and found no difficulty in doing so. How Helen must have loved to find his daily letter on the hall mat in the mornings, uniting them while he was away from home, however briefly. I wondered whether she wrote in response; only Tom's letters to Helen had been retained in the box.

I knew Helen had been a good letter-writer herself from those she sent to us, always in appreciation of a visit, a small gift, or family time shared at our home.

The smallest case held a bundle of certificates; birth, marriage, death, insurance details, house purchase and so forth. Passports were here from early days, with snapshots inside of a handsome young Uncle Tom, and of Aunt Helen, youthful and pretty. So many worldwide stamps in his; so many travels.

Interestingly however, we found nothing at all to do with the baby twins who died early in their marriage, before Malcolm was born. It seemed as if no record was kept of these baby boys at all; perhaps the memory of the loss of them both was too painful to retain.

There were letters in the case tied with faded pale blue ribbon; letters received after Malcolm was born. Such joy, such delight in a new little son, after the tragedy of losing the twins.

'So many friends, Bri,' I commented. 'And all are writing to say how delighted they were to hear the news. Uncle Tom and Aunt Helen were much-loved people, you know. I've always thought of them as a bit distant... remote, really... and yet these letters are evidence of so much love from so many people.'

'Hmm. It's a bit of an eye-opener, isn't it? Just shows, even our own families don't always know who we really are.'

I picked up a small bundle of envelopes held by a rubber band, rotten with age. Its elasticity had gone, and it crumbled in my fingers as I freed the envelopes and looked inside.

'Oh Bri! Here are some from Aunt Helen to Uncle Tom...'

I was so glad to find them; so pleased that she had proclaimed her love for him in response to so much she had received. All the letters were early ones, written before Malcolm had died in 1955. It seemed as if that event had cast such a shadow over their lives that things between them changed for ever afterwards.

These letters were few, written to Uncle Tom when he was away from home on some of his longer business trips, but none of them was long, or indeed as passionate as his had been to her.

The telephone rang in the hall and Brian went to answer it. I could hear through the open door that it was Andrew, and they spoke at length, anxiously, about the failing business.

With half an ear on their conversation, I continued to search through the last of the boxes, and I found the old chocolate box with the picture of the swan on the lid, from Aunt Helen's bedroom drawer. Inside were several small diaries spanning the early years, filled with her tiny writing.

While Brian and Andrew talked, I read the contents of these diaries at random, some telling nothing at all, and one or two telling so much. I put these to one side. What I did notice in particular, was the fact that Aunt Helen had noted dates when Gordon was away on business and when he returned, rather than Uncle Tom. And these entries began in the 1952 diary, three years before Malcolm's death, and the very same year that Gordon's wife Florence had died, of cause unknown.

A chill crept up my spine. We had never discovered the reason for Florence's death; never found a certificate giving a stated cause. It was a mystery, although Paul must have known at the time. What we now knew, however, was that a relationship between Gordon and Aunt Helen had already begun, and despite all their efforts to contain it, did Uncle Tom himself find out? Did he, poor man, continue to send his loving letters for some years to a wife who received them without delight, her heart already with another man?

And did Gordon, besotted as he was with Helen even then, feel unable to mourn the loss of his young wife, and thereby cause an everlasting rift between himself and Paul, who loved Florence dearly?

We were never to know for sure, but my inquisitive mind ran ahead of me once again to what may have been.

'Okay, old son, we'll do that then. I'll speak to you tomorrow. Our love to Mary. Bye.'

Brian returned from the hall and sighed.

'Not good news, I'm afraid. The most recent purchaser has pulled out.'

We were struggling, with Andrew, to find a purchaser for his gym, and these were not easily forthcoming. Liquidation of the business loomed gloomily on the horizon.

'I'll make coffee…'

I jumped up from my position on my knees by the open windows. The sun was going down fast now, and I flicked on the external patio light, illuminating the late spring garden in the evening. Both dogs lay sleeping on the still-warm flagstones of the patio.

'No, no… I'll do it. Actually, I think I'll have a glass of wine; what about you?'

Brian headed for the kitchen and the open bottle of red we had enjoyed with our dinner earlier.

'No, thanks, just coffee. Tell me…'

He proceeded through the hatch to fill me in on the details of the gym, and I felt keenly the stress he and Andrew had shared on the phone.

I packed away the boxes, cases and contents from the floor for another time, leaving Elmwood days behind once more. More pressing concerns were upon us, and the history of the house, even its ongoing mysteries, would have to wait.

Chapter Twenty-one

May proved to be gorgeous, and we ventured out into the old garden at Elmwood one Sunday afternoon when we were there at the house for a final check of all the rooms. At the end of the overgrown garden we could see the river shimmering in the sunshine, and a family of ducks swam past as we stood on the bank. Brian put one arm around my shoulders, and sighed.

'It's so strange to think that soon this place will belong to someone else,' he said wistfully. 'All my life it's been part of our family, somehow, and especially lately, I've had so much involvement here.'

'I know, love. It will seem odd.'

We looked behind us, up the long garden towards the back of the house.

'It's so derelict now; do you think whoever buys this place will rebuild?'

'What, demolish it completely, you mean? I doubt it. Probably just renovate, and repair all the damage done by damp. It'll need a new roof for sure.'

I thought of the day we had been right up in the loft space, finding Uncle Tom's old trunk, and how the wind had whistled through open rafters in the roof. We wandered back up the garden to the house hand in hand, past the old cat shelters, and the metal ladder against the wall. We could only just make out the little graves amidst the tall, overgrown weeds and grasses, where Aunt Helen had buried her beloved cats.

So much history here; such a story. My mind turned to Gordon, and his connections here; and I wondered anew about his poor wife.

'Bri; I've been thinking. You don't suppose... I mean, do you think Gordon could possibly have been responsible for his wife's death?' I suggested, feeling somewhat guilty at the thought. We reached the back door, and on going inside, it was at once dark and gloomy again, as we left the May sunshine behind us.

Brian laughed.

'Good Lord, Mags, are you onto that one again? What makes you think so, even?' he said, locking the back door with the huge old iron key and hanging it back on its nail by the worn string.

'Well,' I pondered. 'It just seems to fit in, somehow. And Florence's death is quite a mystery, really. We've never found anything to answer all my questions about her, have we? All we've got to go on is the document you found stating her grave plot in the cemetery, amongst all those old receipts and things.'

We made our way up to the top of the house, looking into each room and checking that it was clear. There was so much rubbish, so many bits of litter that no one wanted. Once we had made certain that nothing of value remained, Brian was to arrange for final clearance of all this mess to take place, and the house would be put up for sale.

The entrance to the loft space was an eerie hole. Full of thick cobwebs and no doubt spiders, I had avoided coming up here most of the time, leaving the search to Brian in this particular place. It looked as though Gordon had thrown much of his personal junk from his house next door into this place; somewhere no one would see it, and therefore it would not need to be sorted or cleared out. There were more piles of photographic stuff (his old hobby), an old projector and screen, furled like a huge umbrella, and too creased to use. Boxes and boxes of wildlife group papers; garden party details and fund-raising events. Rows of old books on shelves heavy with dust, and...

In one corner, once my eyes had adjusted to the dim light, I could just make out a pink tin. It was fairly large and square, with a picture of flowers on the lid, and it looked as if it had once held biscuits; the sort that you receive at Christmas in a fancy tin.

'Oh, look, Bri; another tin like the McVites one that held those old love letters.' I said, reaching for it bravely, in view of the surrounding cobwebs. I brushed off the surface dirt and we took it downstairs into the light to examine it.

On the old table in the breakfast room – not an antique nor even one of little value for a charity shop – we opened the pink tin to find more letters. Brian laughed.

'Well, would you believe it?' he joked. 'Yet more mail! I think they retained every single bit of post that ever entered this house, you know! What have we here?'

These letters were written on small sheets of paper, the sort one used to buy years ago in a Basildon Bond pad, and the address at the top of the first one was a house in Cornwall. It read:

My dear Gordon,

I'm feeling much better today and have managed to eat a good breakfast; probably because I had a really good night and slept until eight o'clock this morning. It's funny to wake up to the cockerel here, and I do love the countryside. All around us here there are cows and sheep, and Mabel is so kind. She bought a Fullers walnut cake for tea yesterday. Did you tell her it was my favourite?

I'm longing to see you on Saturday when you come. The train gets in around lunchtime, so Mabel says she'll have a ham salad for you. Please would you bring my other slippers... the red ones that match my dressing gown? Tell Paul I love him, and I'm so much better the doctor here says I'll be home in a week or so.

Ever your loving

Florrie

I read the letter aloud, and looked at Brian, fascinated.

'It's from his wife,' I said. 'She must have been ill, and gone to Cornwall for convalescence, like they used to do in those days. D'you think?'

Brian smiled. I knew he was amused by my ponderings and the interest that I had in this scenario.

'Mmm, maybe,' he said, taking the letter from me, and reading it again himself. 'It sounds affectionate, Mags... she must have loved him. What's the date?'

We looked carefully at the postmark on the envelope, as Florrie hadn't written the date inside. September, 1952.

'That's just before she died,' I commented, remembering. 'But she writes that she is better.'

I opened a second letter, written on similar paper, in Florence's writing again. This one was dated only two days later.

Dear Gordon

It's almost Saturday! I can't wait till you come. Please don't bother to bring any more pink sleeping pills from the doctor as I'm sleeping well again and I'm so much stronger now. I'm sure I shan't need those any more. The doctor here is very pleased with me and thinks the operation was a real success. Just one thing though; could you fetch some more library books, as I've almost finished the last Jalna one. Another Whiteoak one would be nice. So little to do all day but read; how I long to come home! Oh well, only a few more days I hope.

With my love, darling,

Florrie

There was one more small letter in Florence's distinctive handwriting, and it was in a very different vein. This time she wrote:

Gordon.

Paul has spoken to me on the phone tonight, and he is so terribly upset. You will know what I mean. I can't find words to tell you what I feel but I'm coming home tomorrow because of it all. I shall need more pink pills after all; I'm sure you'll understand, in view of what's happened and what's been going on, so please arrange for me to have a new prescription for them as soon as I'm home. I'll catch the morning train. Mabel will take me to the station and carry my case so I'll be all right. She can't understand why you aren't coming here after all, but I told her something had come up.

Florrie

'Bri! What about this one!' I almost shouted. It seemed to be a revelation, though all we could do was to read between the lines and probably come up with something quite incorrect. What was definitely clear, from the dramatic difference in the way Florence had addressed Gordon, and signed the letters, was that somehow he had fallen badly out of favour in the course of a couple of days.

I sat heavily on the corner of the old table, feeling a mixture of shock and excitement. Did these letters actually tell us what could have become of poor Florence?

Brian had opened others; letters and cards it would appear, of condolence, and when we checked the dated postmarks, they were written just a week or so later. So Florence had died soon after her final letter, stating that she was coming home from Cornwall.

'Look at this one, Mags,' Brian said, seriously. Gone were his smiles and the laughter at my imaginings. 'It's from Aunt Helen. Just her, though, not from Uncle Tom too. Wouldn't you think it would be from them both?'

We read Aunt Helen's letter; dated 20 September 1952, and written in her tiny writing on a large, thin sheet of paper.

My dearest Gordon,

it read

'The news I have just received is so great a shock I am at a loss to express my feeling. All I can do is to offer my sympathy, and indeed my very great love for you from my heart. You gave Florrie so much, Gordon, and cared for her with devotion. I am sad to learn that she discovered what she did in such a way, and at such a time. Your heart will heal, my darling, and I am here to help you always. Your feelings of guilt will pass, and the memories will fade.

Remember that I love you.

Helen

We were both silent for a moment, stunned with the shock and reality of what we had read.

'Better get home, Mags,' Brian said, after a minute or two. 'I'll come back tomorrow to finish off. There's that chap coming about the piano, so I'll have to be here to show it to him, anyway. I don't feel like doing any more now, do you?'

I shook my head, still stunned. Most unlike me to be silent. We closed the lid of the pink tin and took it home to study further later, and left Elmwood and its horrible secret once more.

Back at home, the phone rang as we opened the front door. It was Louise.

'Hello, Maggie, it's me.' she said. 'I wondered whether you could do the church flowers for me for next weekend? I'm supposed to be doing them, but we've got the chance to go to the New Forest with Tim and Sandra, so I just thought...'

'Yes, of course I will,' I said. 'No problem at all; we're here all weekend. I'll do them on Saturday morning.'

Somehow I couldn't say:

'Guess what we've just discovered?' It all seemed so unreal, and I still felt shocked. Clearly, Aunt Helen's and Gordon's affair was underway when his wife was ill, and it would seem that she found out through poor Paul. No wonder Aunt Helen wrote that letter just from herself, as it was entirely personal, and Uncle Tom didn't feature at all.

I made a pot of tea and we drank it on the patio in the early evening sunshine.

'I feel as though I need a brandy, really,' I smiled. 'It's been quite a shock, finding those letters, hasn't it?'

Brian nodded.

'Puts a different slant on things, I suppose,' he said thoughtfully. 'Do you feel able to look at the rest?'

'Yes, I think we should. I'll get the tin.'

Such an ordinary old tin, somehow, and yet it contained such shocking truths. We found other letters, bunched in an old rubber band, which withered when we removed it from its pile. These were letters of condolence, written to Gordon and Paul in the very week following that first happy letter from Florrie in Cornwall. All of them stated what a shock her sudden death had been; one friend even wrote that she had seen Florrie and talked to her the very day before she died, and that she seemed so much better after her operation.

I put these things together in my inquisitive mind.

'Brian...' (I only used his name in full when I was very serious or formal), 'what do you think of this for an explanation? Florrie had some operation or other and went to Cornwall for convalescence. She recovered really well; so much so that she no longer needed her pink sleeping pills. Then, just before she was expecting Gordon... perhaps to take her home; Paul phoned and told her about his father's affair with Aunt Helen next door! Maybe he even came in and found them together...'

'Stop it, Mags! You're getting carried away...'

'But it could be true! Just imagine… it would upset a lad of what was he, sixteen? So then he phoned Florrie to tell her, and she came home on the train at once, furious and upset with Gordon, to goodness knows what a to-do. She asked for more sleeping pills, although she'd just said she didn't need them any more, and then a few days later, she was dead. And people had seen her, and said she looked well. Perhaps she took an overdose, Bri…'

'Good Lord, Maggie! We don't know that!'

I looked down sheepishly.

'No, I suppose we don't. But it is just possible, you have to admit. And how terrible it would have been to live next door to the very woman who had stolen your husband… a woman who probably had been her friend.'

There were more letters in the tin. One was from Uncle Tom, in his familiar handwriting, but strangely formal. It read:

Dear Lench,

I am at a loss to know how to express my deep distress on hearing the dreadful news of Florence's death this morning. I understand from Helen that she has already written to you, but I must of course, send my own condolences to you and indeed to Paul, who has lost a fine mother, whom he loved dearly. It will be hard for you both, and this time of grieving will be awful for you.
Please allow us to help you in any way possible.

Sincerely,

Tom Fawley

One other letter, conspicuous by its size, and folded three times to fit in the tin, was from the Borough of Barnes. It had a large red seal on it, and was an official letter granting exclusive right of burial in a certain grave section in the nearby cemetery. It named the number, the class and the grave section for Florence Lench.

'Bri… do you think we could find this grave?' I asked. 'I just think it would be interesting to see it… you know, what Gordon had done as an inscription, and so on. There must be a head-stone.'

'Well, we could try, if you like, though I can't see a purpose, myself,' Brian said.

'I just want to find out if she was loved, really,' I said wistfully.

We read the remaining notes and cards in the tin, and put them away, closing the lid on another chapter in the Elmwood saga. But it left us mystified, without the answers that I wanted, and indeed, with more unsolved questions in my head.

Chapter Twenty-two

Staring at me in Brian's office on the Thursday was one last plastic sack, unchecked. It contained the small tan attaché case we had spotted in the loft when we were pulling out Uncle Tom's old trunk, and because it was so filthy I had put it into the sack to protect everything it might subsequently touch. The tan leather was faded and crumbled with the poor, damp conditions in the loft, and its surface turned to dust in my fingers as I took it out of the sack. Brian was sitting at his desk in the office, typing figures into the computer, and he looked up as I struggled with the case.

'The wretched thing's locked, Bri,' I said. 'There's only one catch, and no key.'

He stood up, leaving his screen switched on. This was a working day.

'Don't flap; I'll get my hammer.'

He disappeared to the lobby where his tool box was kept, and returned to find me huffily wiping my hands on an old towel.

'Look at this! The leather is rotten and it's left my hands all brown...'

'Well, you wanted to open the thing, not me,' Brian grumbled. 'Shall we just push it back in the sack and chuck it?'

'No! Oh no... I want to see what's inside.'

One blow of the hammer on the old catch and the little case flew open, scattering yet more letters at my feet. They had aged well, unlike the case, having been well sealed inside, and I picked up the first one to recognise immediately Gordon's distinctive handwriting. In fact, all the envelopes, cards and messages were the same. All written and sent by Gordon... to Aunt Helen. I checked the dates; some were written as early as 1958, and all were loving and passionate.

'I've got to get on, work must be done,' Brian said, resuming his place at the desk, and the computer keys began to click once more.

'Bri, these are all love letters,' I said, removing my glasses. 'All of them. And most were written before... long before... Uncle Tom died. Perhaps that's why the case was in the top loft, out of sight so he didn't find them.'

'Mmm.'

I realised that I had lost Brian's interest, or maybe he wasn't comfortable with this fact that his uncle had been betrayed in his lifetime, and by someone of whom we were also fond. I put the letters back into the case and pushed it into the sack again.

'What should we do with this, then?' I asked.

'Chuck it out, I should think,' came his reply, and so I did.

The evidence was gone, but the fact remained that we had seen for ourselves the affair on paper, and there was no denying the fact that it had really happened. It actually added to my curiosity about poor Florence's death, and I was eager to discover more.

It rained on the Saturday. I bought spray carnations, large pink lilies and armfuls of greenery and gypsophila, and we drove to church to decorate it in the morning. Two large vases later, on the communion table and the large octagonal font under the pulpit, we were ready to go. Brian had been outside chatting to the caretaker while I arranged the flowers, and he fetched the car from the car park when he saw that I was ready.

'Thanks, darling,' I said, jumping in to the passenger seat when he pulled up, to save me getting wet. I shook out my umbrella; it was a really heavy downpour.

'That's another job done. Poor Louise and David, if the weather's like this in the New Forest.'

Brian looked disenchanted with our next plan for the day.

'Do you really want to go cemetery searching in this?' he enquired, clearly hopeful that I would change my mind. But he was out of luck.

'Yes, indeed I do, if you don't mind,' I said eagerly. 'A spot of rain won't hurt us. And anyway, I know exactly where to go now that I've spoken to the girl on the phone.'

I had telephoned the cemetery on the Friday, to check that the document we had was correct, and to ascertain the whereabouts of Florence's grave. A pleasant girl on the telephone told me that yes, Florence Beatrice Lench was buried in grave space section Y, number 204, class B, and there were maps at the cemetery gate to show the location.

We drove up to the gates as the rain began to ease, and I hopped out of the car to collect one of the little maps. It was easy to find the grave, and we walked together through rows of tombstones, reading each one carefully.

I held Brian's hand.

'Look, Bri; some of these are so moving,' I said with emotion. 'I can't bear to think how these poor relatives felt, losing their loved ones, and having them buried here, perhaps on a miserable wet day like today. I much prefer cremation.'

Brian was not in talkative mood, and could no doubt think of a hundred and one things that he would rather be doing, than searching for a fifty-year-old grave in a wet cemetery on a Saturday morning. I read some of the tombstones' inscriptions out loud:

'Edward Pearcy, aged fifty-eight. December 13th 1928. Rest in peace beloved.'

'Sarah Jane Gould, beloved wife of Michael and mother of Thomas and Patricia. Departed this life on August 12th, 1937. Dreadfully missed and loved for ever.'

'Oh, Bri... it's so sad to read these... all people who were loved so much.'

He squeezed my hand, as he peered at each monumental inscription.

'Hmm. Well, it happens, love. I'm just thankful we still have each other.'

I stopped short beside a small, untended and bedraggled looking grave, overgrown with weeds and grass, its small head-stone at a rakish angle against the side wall of the grave. Its inscription read:

'Florence Beatrice Lench.

Aged 43 years.

Died 15th September 1952.'

And that was all.

'This is it! Oh, Bri...' I was emotional and saddened to read so little on a headstone, the last tribute one can give to a loved one.

'Look at this... there's nothing here, nothing to say she was loved, or missed...'

Brian wiped the toppled stone with the side of his shoe, dislodging moss that partially obscured the wording. Nothing more was written beneath.

'It's a crying shame,' he said loudly. 'You're right, Mags; it's not much of an epitaph. And she was still a young woman, so it was a tragedy, really.'

'Not a mention of Gordon, or even Paul,' I said, trying to stand the toppled stone up straight. It refused to budge, having probably laid at an angle for so many years.

'I wonder whether either of them ever came to see this grave, after she was buried?' I said. 'To lay flowers, or tidy the weeds? And it's not much of a grave, even, is it? Gordon with all his money, and he didn't pay for a nice tombstone or anything. I think it's so sad.'

We walked quietly away, back to the car, past just a few people who had come to the cemetery to tend their own small plots. An elderly man, carrying a pot of miniature roses, passed us on the path, and tipped his hat to me with a little smile. A young couple were comforting each other beside a new grave; a mound of earth still, covered with wreaths and flowers from a funeral service probably just days before.

Brian and I reached our car and drove quietly home, deeply sorry for a woman of just forty-three years old, who had died suddenly and tragically, betrayed by the man she had clearly loved so much.

Chapter Twenty-three

I called one afternoon to read the meters again at Elmwood, following a plea from Frank Willis on the telephone. Apparently the previous reading, made by Sally, had gone missing, and as she was on holiday, Frank wondered whether I would be so kind.

It was a beautiful May day, and in the overgrown garden blue-bells had suddenly bloomed in the shade of the old trees, looking for all they were worth as if life continued at the old, gloomy house. The curtains remained closed, to prevent squatters from peering inside, and realising that this was an empty property. How, I wondered, could anyone contemplate moving in here, amidst such filth and squalor? It seemed a sure enough sign that the house was uninhabited, just to look at the shabby wooden barricade against the door.

Inside, a low-wattage bulb burned without even a shade in the hall, and I made my way carefully over the scattered rubbish from our partial clearance, to the cupboard under the stairs which housed the meters.

It was eerily quiet. Inside the cupboard I saw shredded paper in a heap, indicating the presence of rats. No doubt a new infestation, since the removal of dear old Coco to her new home. I hastily checked the meter readings, recorded them on my notepad, and left the cupboard hurriedly, avoiding any disturbance to the paper nest. With a shudder I closed the door firmly, but avoided taking a deep breath due to the putrid air.

Just before I left the house I took a quick look inside the dining room door, to check that all was well and undisturbed since our last visit. Quite obviously someone, probably Sally, had been in from the Cats' Charity at some point, as the old remaining boxes and unwanted goods of Gordon's had been stacked carefully against one wall.

All the antiques had now been removed for auction, the proceeds of which, with the exception of one clock each for Brian and Louise, would go entirely to the Cats' Charity.

Somehow the house seemed so bare, despite the remaining litter and rubbish which had been left unwanted by anyone. I randomly checked the stack of Gordon's old belongings by the wall, and my eyes were drawn to a bright orange carrier bag, containing yet more letters…

They were clearly not as old as the ones we had been reading at home; in fact, as I pulled them out to see closely in the dim, curtained light, I saw that they were mostly unopened, and to my horror that many were in my own handwriting, or easily recognisable, in that of Louise, or our children.

I pushed them all hastily back into the lurid bag and hurried to my car, wanting to be away from the horrors of the house. All the way home, the orange carrier bag stared at me in my rear-view mirror from its position on the back seat, unnerving me somewhat as I drove.

So unsettled was I, that pulling in awkwardly to our front driveway, I clipped the brickwork of the low wall and dislodged my wing mirror. Brian, working in his office at the front, must have heard the crunch, and he hurried outside to meet me as I climbed out of the car.

'Mags! What happened? How did you?…' He held the hanging mirror lovingly in one hand.

'I don't know,' I sighed guiltily. 'I must have pulled in wrongly or something… it just seemed to drop off… '

'Drop off? It can't just drop off! You must have—'

'Well, I'm sorry. I thought I was clear of the wretched wall.'

Out of character for me, I began to sob. Tears are not things I shed easily when things go wrong; rather the 'stiff upper lip, put on a brave face' kind of response from me as a rule.

Brian dropped the mirror and hugged me gently.

'Ssh… it's okay, darling, it's okay.' He kissed my hair. 'It's only a silly wing mirror, after all.'

'But I'm not usually careless!' I cried, and Brian grinned.

'Never!' he said. 'This sort of thing generally just comes off in your hand…'

An old family joke, and it made me smile as I dried my tears.

'I blame it on *that*,' I said, pointing at the orange bag, as between us we removed my shopping, and the notebook containing the Elmwood meter readings.

'I found it at the house.'

'What's in it?'

'I'm not entirely sure, but it's upset me, anyway,' I said, following Brian into the house and closing the door. The dogs raced to greet me, cheering me with their busy little tails.

'It looks like all our letters to Aunt Helen, probably when she was ill,' I said, kicking off my shoes.

Brian emptied the orange bag onto our large kitchen table, and envelopes and postcards spilled out, several of which I recognised from eight years before.

'Look, Bri! Would you believe?... These haven't even been opened!'

Brian looked serious; no flicker of his warm smile on his face, as he checked the sealed envelopes, mostly in my writing, and some in Louise's.

'You're right, they've been withheld, I'd say.' He opened one, and together we read my letter, dated September, and we calculated it to have been in 1995, the autumn before Aunt Helen's death.

In the letter I was writing to express concern for her, knowing she was sick in bed with tuberculosis, and unable to have visitors.

'We are very anxious about you,' I wrote, 'and I've phoned several times this week but you haven't been well enough to take the calls. Gordon tells me you are confined to bed but that he is looking after you, as I'm sure he is doing, very well.

I'm so sorry not to be able to see you or talk to you on the phone, but of course we do understand that you aren't feeling strong enough for visitors or calls. We just hope you will feel much, much better soon...'

'She never saw my letters!' I exclaimed, and Brian put a hand on my shoulder, sensing my distress. Another, and yet another came from the pile on the table, all unopened, all unread.

'Why, Bri? Why did Gordon keep them from her?'

He looked thoughtful, and more than a little angry.

'I bet I know why,' he said, frowning. 'It will all have been part of that manipulation of the will, won't it? Not long after these were all written, Gordon changed Aunt Helen's will, and I'm certain that she wasn't aware of what he was up to.'

'You mean… if she thought we'd all abandoned her, she would more willingly have cut us all out of her will…'

'Exactly. Do you remember that time I saw her in bed and she asked where we had all been? Why we hadn't contacted her? I didn't understand then; thought she was just muddled; but now…'

He fingered the letters on the table, clearly distressed.

'Oh Bri! She never knew how we did care when she was ill!'

'I doubt if Gordon ever told her we had phoned, you know, Mags, although he said he would; I expect he never mentioned a single call.'

'How wicked! To deny her all this…'

I picked up a postcard, sent by James from a holiday abroad.

'And not to allow her even the knowledge of her family's love for her at the end!'

'All part of his plan to cut us all out, I reckon.'

Brian, still looking angry, put on the kettle for our usual restorative cup of tea. I was tidying away the letters from the table; horrified and saddened by what Gordon had done just before Aunt Helen's death, when she had so badly needed us and the knowledge of our love and concern.

All the mail was dated in the last months of her life, from August onwards, when the doctor had told us there was very little time left. This must have been the time when Gordon planned his future in the house, and in order to arrange it all without any interference from the family, he connived to cut us out, both in the will, and as far as he could from Aunt Helen's mind and thoughts. He would certainly have known our various handwriting, as we had all sent him cards at Christmas for some years.

We pushed the carrier bag to one side, and I started to unpack my shopping, while Brian made the tea. Lucy and Daniel were coming to supper, and I had a meal to prepare.

They arrived after work; Lucy weary from a long day at the hospital where she was a physiotherapist, and Daniel late after a particularly long and difficult day in the office. We all 'unwound' in the garden over a glass of wine… beer in Daniel's case… while my lamb casserole finished cooking and the potato dish turned golden brown in the oven.

I told Lucy the tale of the carrier bag.

'Mum! How dreadful! How dare he?' she began. 'I wrote to Aunt Helen; did you find my letters too?'

I shrugged, uncertain, but said that yes, I did think there were a couple of envelopes in her handwriting amongst the pile. She hurried into the kitchen and fetched the bag, and soon the cards and letters were spread out once more, this time on the grass, in the weak, early evening sunshine.

'Look! Here's one!' Lucy opened the envelope and pulled out her letter. 'I remember sending this,' she said as she read. 'I put in this little card, look… with a sweet kitten on it and a little verse… Oh, Mum, she never even saw it!'

Daniel, never having known Aunt Helen, was less disturbed. He began to play ball with the dogs, and Lucy joined me on the long swing seat to read our letters. Brian went to open the wine for our meal, and I sighed.

'Oh well, love,' I said to Lucy, 'as Dad would say, it can't be helped now. Nothing to be done about it; life goes on. But I am sorry Aunt Helen died thinking we had forgotten her, or that we just didn't care.'

Lucy looked thoughtful.

'What I don't understand,' she said, sipping her wine, 'is why Gordon did it? If he loved Aunt Helen so much, why did he cause her to be so hurt and sad? Wouldn't it have been much nicer for her to have our letters and phone calls, when we weren't allowed to visit, and for her to feel loved at the end?'

'Well yes, it certainly would, but…'

'It would have made it more difficult for Gordon to alter the will,' Brian added, returning from the kitchen.

Lucy snorted.

'It's disgraceful,' she said. 'Something should have been done about that man!'

'Too late now, darling,' Brian said. 'No use crying over spilt milk.'

Lucy smiled.

'Mum said you'd say something like that,' she chuckled. 'So predictable, Dad.'

I left them to the shared joke and went to serve the meal. Daniel joined me in the kitchen, to help.

'Sorry, love,' I apologised. 'All this family stuff; Elmwood, and Aunt Helen… you don't know about all of this and it must be so boring. So sorry.'

I gave him a tray of dishes to take through to the dining room for me. It wasn't quite warm enough that evening to eat outside.

'Don't worry, Maggie,' he said with a gentle smile. 'It's all part of marrying into a family, I guess. Okay by me.'

How fortunate we were, I thought, straining vegetables, to have such lovely partners for our children. All dear people, and so caring for us as well. We were indeed, I considered, a lucky family; rich in the things that mattered most, if not in wealth and money. And there, in comparison, had been Gordon, financially so well off, but unloved and unloving at the end. I knew which I would rather be, and I served our meal with a contented smile.

Chapter Twenty-four

The summer continued, and our work at Elmwood was over. The auction took place, and further substantial proceeds were realised from the Fawley family treasures, all for the Cats' Charity, to add to the large legacy they had already received; and the sale of Elmwood was yet to come.

Gordon Lench's estate was wound up finally, to the value of two million pounds for the RSPCA. And Andrew's gym, with all our financial input, as well as his own and Mary's, was in liquidation… a total loss of all we had for the four of us.

Our house was up for sale. Our much-loved family home, where all our children had grown up, and married, before setting out on lives of their own. Our future was frighteningly uncertain.

What, I often wondered, would Aunt Helen think, if she knew now the situation we were in? If she had known, when Auntie Pearl had needed care in the last year of her life, and eventually died unwell in a hospital bed, without the financial support from Aunt Helen, for which she had previously been so grateful?

What a year it had been, discovering as we had done, the secrets of Brian's family history, and realising the consequences suffered, due to the horrendous actions of one old man.

And Elmwood; such a beautiful and cherished family home. I thought back to the days of twinkling lights and roaring fires at Christmas, and happy parties, with all the family together. What a transformation had taken place in the years since Aunt Helen's death, to a place of squalor and degradation. No more were there cats rescued and loved back to health and silky fur; no more were tiny fledglings nurtured when they fell from their nests in the woodland garden, leading down to the river. Now it was overgrown with tangled weeds and high grasses, and the river beyond flowed by almost unseen.

What of the years of love and happiness with Uncle Tom, and Malcolm as an adored little son? Where did all the joy go? How could it have happened, that Helen should begin to love the rogue next door, and when Malcolm's untimely death shook his father beyond recognition, did she turn to Gordon for the comfort that Tom was unable to give?

And then there were those years of secret liaison; the ladder over the wall, the shared meals at Elmwood, the joint love of all animals and the exception of interest in people? Gordon, the cruel and manipulative neighbour, who became to Helen only, so gentle and loving. And yet, never warm towards others; disliked by everyone he met and resigned to his last lonely years with only the company of his cat Coco.

That is, until Trevor Hill 'happened' along and took up residence, even claiming 'squatter's rights' after Gordon's death.

What a story, what a saga. What a history the walls of Elmwood held; what a tale it could have told. We had only glossed over the surface.

As I drove over Putney Bridge one afternoon recently, a beautiful, wide, golden Lexus car edged past me on the inside lane. I caught a clear view of the driver, who looked my way as though he recognised me, or maybe my car.

A dapper-looking gentleman, he was certainly in keeping with his grand and glamorous car; but there was something about his expression, possibly his shifty eyes, that was familiar. One corner of his mouth turned up slightly in a crooked grin as he looked my way.

Was it... could it *possibly* have been Trevor Hill?

TM00708588

Printed in the United Kingdom
by Lightning Source UK Ltd.
108531UKS00001B/127-144

9 781844 015429